MONEY IN THE GRAVE

Lock Down Publications and Ca$h
Presents
MONEY IN THE GRAVE
A Novel by *Martell "Troublesome" Bolden*

Lock Down Publications
Po Box 944
Stockbridge, Ga 30281

Visit our website @
www.lockdownpublications.com

First Edition August 2021
Printed in the United States of America

Lock Down Publications
Like our page on Facebook: Lock Down Publications @
www.facebook.com/lockdownpublications.ldp

Book interior design by: **Shawn Walker**
Edited by: **Shamika Smith**

Stay Connected with Us!

Text **LOCKDOWN** to 22828 to stay up-to-date with new releases, sneak peaks, contests and more...
Thank you.

Submission Guideline.

Submit the first three chapters of your completed manuscript to ldpsubmissions@gmail.com, subject line: Your book's title. The manuscript must be in a .doc file and sent as an attachment. Document should be in Times New Roman, double spaced and in size 12 font. Also, provide your synopsis and full contact information. If sending multiple submissions, they must each be in a separate email.

Have a story but no way to send it electronically? You can still submit to LDP/Ca$h Presents. Send in the first three chapters, written or typed, of your completed manuscript to:

LDP: Submissions Dept
Po Box 944
Stockbridge, Ga 30281

DO NOT send original manuscript. Must be a duplicate.

Provide your synopsis and a cover letter containing your full contact information.

Thanks for considering LDP and Ca$h Presents.

Martell "Troublesome" Bolden

PROLOGUE

Sitting inside the Nissan Maxima in the parking lot of Popeye's, Don and Rich were counting out the re-up money while they awaited the plug. They were dope boys, and money was their motive, even though the half key of yae they were copping between them wouldn't bring in much of it. But they had great expectations, as long as they played the game right.

Don, occupying the driver's seat, glanced down at the re-up money in his lap, then said, "Listen, it's time we start gettin' some real paper because what we been gettin' ain't enough."

"Fa sho. What's the plan?" Rich replied from the passenger seat.

"I plan to talk to the plug about frontin' us a brick, and then we can start by floodin' the hood with work. And after we put the hood on lock, then we'll expand our operations throughout the streets."

"Then let's make the streets ours."

Don looked forward to discussing business with the plug, Ness. The way Don saw it is all they needed was a brick to get started, and then he and Rich, along with their gang, could flip it and get their money and weight up in no time. Rich was all for it, even if it came with beef. He understood that they couldn't beef and get money at the same time. However, Rich knew beef was bound to take place where there was money involved.

Shortly thereafter, Don and Rich noticed Ness's red Cadillac Escalade pulling into the parking lot where it parked beside their Maxima. While Don stepped out of the car, Rich remained inside. Don entered the passenger seat of the Escalade.

"What's good, homeboy?" Don greeted.

"You know me, gettin' to the money," Ness replied.

"Speakin' of, I got a proposal that will benefit us both on the money tip."

"Now you talkin' my language. I'm listenin'."

"Instead of what I came to cop, how 'bout you front me and my gang with a brick?"

Ness leaned back in his cream leather interior seat, caressing his goatee. "Let's say I do front you a brick, then what?"

"Then I make us both richer. Look," Don shifted toward him, "I'm just tryna get my money and weight up in this game."

"A'ight. I'll front you a brick." Ness grinned, displaying his diamond-flooded teeth. "But I want forty Gs for the front durin' your next re-up," he laid out.

"Done."

Ness went into his trap compartment and pulled out a kilo, which he then handed over to Don. After they dapped, Don departed the whip, and as he made his way back towards the Maxima, Ness pulled the Escalade out of the parking lot going on his way. Once Don entered the Maxima, he tossed the kilo into Rich's lap, who grinned.

"Now it's time we get rich off the game," Don said.

Rich looked over at him and replied, "Just remember the game comes with wins and losses."

•••

Sitting inside the Lexus SUV, which was parked on a side street of the suburbs, Rob, TJ, and Max were each masked up and strapped while awaiting their next mark. They were jack-boys, and together they were responsible for laying down many dope-boys throughout the streets. They came up in the game by way of ski masks and blood money. Rob, occupying the passenger seat, glanced down at the FN handgun in his lap and said, "Look, we need to hit a major lick because the ones we been hittin' ain't shit."

"I'm down," TJ said from the driver's seat.

"What do you have in mind?" Max wanted to know. He sat in the backseat.

"First, we need to find a nigga to lurk on that's holdin' more weight than we've ever came up on and strip his ass for everything. Then we'll sell the work for the low in the streets. We'll get paid even if we have to make the streets bleed murder."

Rob wanted to hit a major lick in order to make a fast come-up. The way he saw it was all they needed to do was to catch a drug boss slippin' in order for him and his gang to get rich quick. No one outside of their small gang knew that they were the ones behind the masks and triggers because they almost always murked their marks. And Rob wanted to keep it that way.

Shortly after that, Rob and his gang observed the red Cadillac-Escalade pull up and park outside the stash house. They peeped Ness step out of the Escalade with a duffel bag and then enter the redbrick home. Rob, TJ, and Max hopped out of the SUV with guns in hand and hurried towards the stash house's front door. Violently, Rob kicked in the door, and then TJ and Max barged inside, finding Ness seated on the couch before a coffee table which was covered with two bricks of yay and numerous stacks of money. Not to mention a handgun that was cocked and loaded. While Rob leveled his FN on Ness, Max began to hurriedly toss the goods from the coffee table into the duffel, making sure to take every-thing, and TJ checked out the rest of the house.

"Where the fuck is the rest of the stash at?!" Rob demanded to know.

Ness leaned back on the brown leather couch. "Just take what's there and leave. It's more than enough," he bargained.

Rob hissed, "Nigga, I ain't gonna ask you again!"

Boc! Boc! Boc! Boc!

Rob popped Ness in the face and chest before Ness could even respond. Almost instantly, Ness died from the impact of the slugs ripping through main organs, and blood poured out of his wounds as he looked to be asleep while sitting up. Leaving their mark dead, Rob, TJ, and Max rushed out of the stash house and back to the Lex', then they skirted off down the street.

Rob pulled off his mask and smirked, "That's how you put in work." He was riding shotgun.

"Shit was light work," Max replied as he pulled the mask up on his head like a ski cap. He was in the back with the duffel bag beside him. "Nigga didn't even know what was comin'."

"Niggas should know better than to be lackin' in these streets with goons lurkin'," TJ added as he swerved around a vehicle in traffic. He steered towards their routine spot, which was the seedy Diamond Inn motel. "Didn't have to murk the nigga though, Rob."

Rob eyed TJ through slits. "You know the rules: murk 'em all and keep movin'."

CHAPTER 1

In the kitchen of the trap house, Don and Rich were along with their gang; T-Mac, C-Note, and Danger. The gang had grown up together in the same hood. They had each other's backs. Their plan was to rise to power and become one of the biggest drug organizations in the city of Milwaukee. And they knew that would come with niggas praying on their downfall. Although, they understood that together they were a force to be reckoned with. Over time, they planned to have their hood sewed up, starting with the brick they had gotten on front. They would be ready to expand their operations throughout the streets and begin to make a way out of no way. Aside from possible beef, the only problem was they needed supply to keep up with the demand.

Don and Rich were brothers. Even though Don was the oldest, he often treated Rich like a homeboy. And T-Mac was their cousin who normally hung around with Rich. As for C-Note and Danger, they had both grown up more so homeboys with Don. Being that each of them were dope-boys, they banded together to form their small gang. And though they were about trappin' off the dope, that didn't mean they wouldn't settle for blood on the dope.

The gang sat at the worn kitchen table. They had the table covered with stacks of cash, drug paraphernalia, and their guns. They were putting in a day's work.

"Fucked up how Ness went out," Don said and shook his damn head while he was counting up profits made throughout the day.

"Well, he won't be needin' any money in the grave." Don was tall and pudgy with a tan hue, light brown eyes, and a bald fade haircut. Twenty-nine years of age, Don was a young street nigga. He had been trying to make enough paper to move out the hood. First, he wanted to put his hood on lock by any means.

Rich sat beside him wrapping stacks of cash with rubber bands. "Nigga got caught slippin'. That's why it's best to just keep a low profile so not to draw attention from the jackboys." Favoring his brother's skin complexion and eyes, Rich was slimmer and a few inches shorter. He had his hair done into a man-bun and only had a peach fuzz of a goatee. Normally the type of nigga to keep a cool head, so whenever Rich loses his cool, he was quick to bust his heat.

"Well, I won't be caught slippin' in these streets," Don assured.

"Any word on who robbed and killed Ness?" Danger asked no one in particular while weighing up the work. He held a stalky build with a bronze tone and a bald head. Danger had been in the game long enough to know that the days were numbered, which is why he wasn't afraid to ride or die on any given day.

"No word at all. Whoever it was got away," T-Mac piped in as he bagged up the yae. Athletically built and average in height, he was brown skin with low brush waves. And T-Mac didn't mind bagging up dope or body bagging an opp.

"So, them niggas still out in the streets lurkin'," Rich mentioned.

"And they bet not try a nigga like me," Don stated.

"Look, now that Ness is gone, we'll need another plug," C-Note chimed in while standing in the kitchen at the stove cooking up the latest batch of product on a Pyrex. Standing tall with a slender build, he was light skin with dreadlocks draping to his mid-back. His tatts and gold teeth couldn't go unnoticed. C-Note was a pistol-toting dope boy.

"Already have a plug on deck," Don told them. "This nigga named Castle, who I met a while back at the gamble spot. I'm sure he'll be able to flood us with work."

C-Note halted cooking up the crack and looked to him. "Then set up a buy from this Castle nigga. We gonna need as much work as we can get if we gonna sew up the hood."

"The problem with that is we're bound to have beef over the hood with Heavy and his boys," Rich added.

"That nigga, Heavy, and his boys can get it," Danger asserted.

"And we can ride out on them niggas tonight," T-Mac agreed.

"All that'll cause is ongoing' beef," C-Note said.

Rich looked around the room and said, "We can't beef and get money."

"Rich has a point," Don second. "I'll meet with Heavy and try to get him on board with us."

There was a knock at the front door, and T-Mac went to answer it. Once he pulled open the door, he found a thin, disheveled woman who was a crackhead. She was actually Don and Rich's mom, Angie. Ever since her sons could remember, she'd been heavily on crack, and she'd do just about anything to get her next high. She was in her mid-forties and had been chasing a high for years. Though she was an addict, one could tell she was once a good-looking lady, having the same complexion and eyes as her two boys. Angie's sons didn't like seeing her high on crack, and even though they distributed the very drug that destroyed her life, they tried convincing her to get clean. However, getting her out of the hood was the motive.

T-Mac stepped aside and said, "C'mon in, Auntie Angie."

"Where are my boys?" Angie asked as she stepped inside, and T-Mac closed the door behind her.

13

"They're in the kitchen. Auntie, you know they don't like seein' you this way. Why don't you just come back another time." T-Mac could tell Angie was high, and he knew Don and Rich disapproved of her drug abuse. It was tough on him seeing her strung out because Angie was his favorite auntie.

"T-Mac, whether they like it or not, I'm still their damn mama." Angie turned for the kitchen with T-Mac trailing her, shaking his head.

Don looked up and seen Angie. "Ma, thought I told you not to come here. And are you high right now?" he said disapprovingly.

"Don, why don't you just lemme live my life? I ain't here to have you lecture me," Angie retorted.

"Then why are you here? 'Cause all I can guess is that you want somethin'." Rich snorted.

Angie attempted to fix her poorly kept hair. "I just need a hit to get by, and then I'll leave you two alone."

"All you give a fuck about is gettin' high. You were never here for us, so we're used to you leavin' us alone." Rich resented her for choosing to be an addict over being a mom.

"Be easy, Rich." Don looked to the others and told them, "Give us a moment." All but Don, Rich, and Angie cleared out the kitchen. Don grabbed a piece of crack, stepped over to his mom, and handed it to her. "Ma, listen, I won't keep feedin' your habit. This will be the last time. One of these days, you gonna have to get clean so you can live a better life."

"And one of these days, I will," Angie promised. She hugged Don and then tried offering Rich a peck on the cheek, which he held up a hand to decline. Angie turned and headed out of the trap.

Rich jumped to his feet. "I'ont get why you give her ass anything if you want her to get clean."

"Don't you realize if she doesn't get it from us, then she'll just get it from someone else?" Don reasoned. "Rich, she needs our help getting' clean. I don't know about you, but I'ma do whatever I can for her. I know how you feel about her, but don't you forget she's still our mom."

"And don't you forget she's not the one who raised us; it was the streets." Rich took a seat back at the table and continued wrapping up stacks of cash.

Don also took his seat. "At least she loves us. The streets love none."

•••

Heavy scooped some coke from one of the kilos with his long, dirty pinky nail, lifted it to his nostril, and powdered his nose. The two keys sat atop the pool table along with stacks of cash and a couple of pistols. While Heavy stood near the pool table, his underboss, Swindle, was seated on a bar stool at the wet bar. A few of their hitters lounged around, awaiting their next command. They were in their trap spot in the hood inside the basement where the space was setup similar to a sports bar, with a wet-bar kiddie cornered, the pool table in the center of the floor, and the 60" flat-screen TV mounted on the wall before the huge cream-colored leather sectional couch. Not to mention there was the stench of weed and liquor.

"Shit's cut, but it's good," Heavy said and then sniffed a few times due to the cocaine's effect. He was large in the game, running his own crew, and was the plug for lots throughout his hood. A big man, standing at 6'5" with a heavy build and in his late thirties. He was brown-skinned with a bald head and goatee. His motive was money, which also could be his motive to kill.

"I'm sure whoever these bricks came from woulda taxed us much more for 'em," Swindle commented. He'd started out as one of Heavy's hitters, and after proving that he was about whatever, Heavy then decided to take Swindle under him. Swindle was high-yellow in complexion with tatts all over, including one on his baby face. He stood average in height with a stalky build and wore his hair cut into a nappy Philly-fro. In his mid-twenties, Swindle had been playing the game since his early teen years. And over the years, he'd learned to play for keeps, even if that meant taking a nigga out the game.

"Then it's a good thing we were able to cop these blocks for cheap. That's the price of blood on the dope," Heavy said, wearing a smirk.

"Thing is, I'ont trust anything cheap because there's always a strong possibility that whatever it is can become a problem in the long run."

"Swindle, you just don't trust who the bricks came from, is all. But don't trip. If it becomes any problem, then we'll solve it by any means necessary. Now we can flood the hood with more work."

"As long as we can put some weight in all of our main trappers' hands, then we're bound to sew up the hood."

Swindle took a swig from his glass of Remy. "And what about our other problem? You can't think Don n'em are just gonna stand back and allow us to control the drug flow in the hood without makin' a move of their own."

"Don's in no position to make any moves as of now. Definitely since the nigga Ness, who he was coppin' weight from, got murked. Now Don n'em will be lookin' to find a replacement plug in order to re-up on product. And while they're doin' that, we'll just recruit some of their trappers and make 'em work for us."

"It won't take long for Don to find another plug, especially since he's a known Trap God. Any plug will flood him with product. So, it's best that we just take Don out before he becomes a bigger problem," Swindle suggested. He knocked back the remains of his glass.

Heavy picked up a stack of the cash from the pool table and then leafed through its bills. *More money, more problems*, he thought to himself while shaking his head. Looking over to his underboss, Heavy said, "If Don gives us any problems, then we'll take him out. For now, let's focus on gettin' money." He turned to two of his hitters. "Y'all niggas go cook up this dope and then distribute it to the traps that are low on product. In the meanwhile, me and Swindle will finish countin' up this money."

After the two hitters collected the blocks and went to do as told, Heavy and Swindle were left calculating the latest gains from one of their few trap houses throughout the hood. While Heavy fed the money counter with bills, Swindle wrapped each calculated stack with rubber bands. They were bound to get blood on their hands, being that they were counting blood money.

•••

Rob, TJ, and Max were in a crummy motel room at the Diamond Inn. After dumping off the keys for the low that they had come up on from the lick on Ness, they were there dividing their gains. The gang of bandits were seated at the table, hand counting the dividends as they passed around a blunt.

In the beginning, the gang had started out with just Rob and Max hittin' petty licks. When they wanted to pull off bigger capers, they brought TJ and, lastly, their apprehended comrade, Bone, into the fold. And since then, the gang has been avid jack-boys throughout the streets. So much so that law enforcers and outlaws alike were out to put an end to their money, mayhem, and murder. Depending on who caught them first would determine whether they may be buried in a cell or in a grave. But no one outside of their small gang could really say who was behind the masks and triggers. Because, for the most part, they had been meticulous and almost always murked their marks. So, the only way they would be caught was if either of them were caught slippin'.

"Been thinkin' about our next move, and I think it'll be big for us," Rob said and then puffed the blunt. He was a brown-skinned nigga with an average build. His hair was cut into a bald fade, and tatts covered his arms. Even though Rob was like the leader of the gang, he didn't mind allowing his boys to take the lead whenever one of them felt the need to. He was a reasonable nigga, but if given a reason, he would be quick to murk anyone without thinking twice.

"What's the move?" Max asked. He had light brown eyes which matched his complexion, and his dread locks were shoulder length. Though he was shorter than the others, he had just as much heart. Max was down to ride and loyal to the gang.

"The gamble spot. There's always major paper comin' in and goin' out. Plus, while I observed the spot, I noticed on certain days, it doesn't have enough security to keep eyes on everyone. It won't be a problem for the three of us to lay it down."

"And when are we gonna lay down this spot?" TJ wanted to know. He was a dark-skinned, slim nigga with low waves. TJ was reserved yet quick on the trigger.

"Sunday night," Rob answered. "It's when the spot is mostly packed. So that gives us three days to case the spot and come up with a game plan. We'll each stakeout and case the spot for a night, and then compare notes the night before the lick."

"I'll take tonight," Max volunteered.

"And I'll stake out tomorrow night," TJ offered.

"Then I'll do the night before we move," Rob accepted. "We're bound to come outta that bitch with upwards to a hundred Gs." He hit the blunt once more before passing it to his right to Max.

Max scoffed. "That isn't enough money."

"What, can't make your cut of the cash here last? It seems like it's never enough money with you, Max," TJ jabbed.

"TJ, too much money ain't enough money." Max pulled on the weed. "And I'm willin' to kill whoever gets in the way of me gettin' as much money as possible," he asserted.

"It's thinkin' like that which caused Bone to get greedy and almost get all of us ended," TJ sniped.

"Leave Bone outta this. All I'm sayin' is if we're gonna hit licks, great risks come with great reward."

"And all I'm sayin' is I ain't willin' to risk my freedom or life outta greed."

Rob decided to intervene: "Both of you niggas have a point. We do need a major lick, but we don't need to get greedy. When somethin' comes up, then we'll focus on that. For now, let's stay focused on the gamble spot." He pushed each of their cuts of the take in front of them. "Be ready to mask up and rob and kill."

•••

Subsequent to leaving the motel, Rob made his way to the graveyard in his matte black Dodge Challenger Hellcat on Forgiato rims. The cemetery was scarce on this chilly, fall night, and the only light shone down was from the hovering crescent moon.

With a brown paper bag in one hand and a shovel in the other, Rob stood at the burial grounds. After every lick, he would bury money away. It was his way of safekeeping, and he had been doing this for years. He chose the graveyard because it was the last place anyone would think to look for buried money.

No one else knew about the money in the grave. Not even his gang. It wasn't that he didn't trust any of them to know; it was just he trusted them with his life more than with his money. Though he didn't think any of them would ever betray him over money, he also understood that money could turn friends into enemies. So, he rather keep his friends and money separate in order to keep them both. No matter what, money can't buy real friends.

Rob dropped the bag filled with money at his feet and began digging up the burial grounds. The shovel scraped against the ground as it plunged into the dirt. He was sure not to bury the money too deep. His stash was approximately three feet below the earth. Once he dug deep enough, the shovel made a thud against the wooden box in the soil. He used his hands to remove the rest of the dirt from atop the box, and once he pulled open its top, there were numerous stacks of cash inside. Thus far, there was nearly seven-hundred grand. And tonight, he'd be adding forty Gs more. His goal was a million dollars, and then he planned to get out of the stickup game. Until then, it was the ski mask way.

After placing the stacks of cash he had brought along inside the box with the rest of the stacks, Rob recovered the burial grounds with dirt. He grabbed up the emptied bag and the shovel, then headed for his Hellcat. As he drove out of the graveyard, his mind was focused on his next lick. As much as he didn't mind masking up and robbing and killing for the money, he would rather not have to be doing these anymore. Rob needed a lick that would be big enough for him and his crew to come up on just enough money to change their lives. He always understood that when it comes to money, just enough will solve your problems, and too much will kill you.

Martell "Troublesome" Bolden

CHAPTER 2

Mayfair mall was filled with shoppers coming and going by the droves. Don was there to meet with the plug, Castle. Castle had picked the meeting grounds. He liked to meet in public places in case a nigga had the idea to jack him. Don didn't mind it because he was there strictly on business. This was the first the two were meeting to do a deal.

Don, along with C-Note and Danger, made their way through the food court where Castle was awaiting. Once Don spotted Castle seated at a table alone as he made his way over, he took notice of the four goons sitting closely by at separate tables. While Don approached the table, C-Note and Danger hung back. Don took a seat before Castle.

"I heard you're good for business," Castle opened. He was brown-skinned with a trim build, fresh low cut, and hazel eyes. And at thirty-four years of age, he was established. He was the connect for many of the dealers throughout the Mil. And though he happened to make it out of the trenches, he never forgot where he came from.

"And I heard the same about you," Don replied.

Castle leaned back in his seat and studied Don. "Look, if we're gonna do business, then make sure you come with your money right. A'ight."

"No problem. You just make sure the dope is good."

"Speakin' of both, there's yours." Castle nodded towards the Foot Locker bag atop the table. Don checked inside the bag and discovered the two keys within the shoebox. "Now, where's mine?" he asked, and Don then fished out a brown paper bag from his pocket and slid it across the table. Castle peeped inside the bag and saw the stacks of cash but didn't even bother to count it before pocketing it. Whenever making a deal, he never wanted to look suspect.

"I expect that the money is right. If not, then let this be our first and last time doin' business."

Don grabbed up the Foot Locker bag and stood. "In that case, then I'll be in touch to do more business with you soon, as long as the dope is good." He turned on his way, flanked by C-Note and Danger.

Now that the gang had a plug, it was time for them to get their money and weight up in the game. However, if they didn't play the game right, then it could be game over.

•••

Heavy set on the couch watching a boxing match while Swindle shot a game of pool with one of the hitters. They were in their trap spot located in the hood inside the basement. Another one of the hitters came escorting a nigga from around the hood named Trip, along with his mans, Coop, into the basement area.

"Just the niggas that I wanna see," Heavy mused as he took a puff of the blunt.

Trip was a skinny, dark skin nigga with beady eyes, buckteeth, and short dreadlocks. He was about his money and had Coop put in gun work. Coop had a brown complexion, chunky, and rocked a hi-top fade. He had Trip's back. Trip and Coop were moving work for Don's gang, and they were doing numbers, so Heavy wanted parts of that.

"Yo Trip, why don't you take a seat," he directed, and Trip followed while Coop remained standing. With the hitters clutching their poles, neither Trip nor his mans wanted any problems with Heavy. Not to mention Swindle stood on point with a Tec .9 dangling from around his neck by its strap on full display.

"Heard you wanna holla at me. So, what's this about?" Trip wanted to know.

"It's about money. Look, I'ma hit you with a brick, and all I want is thirty-two Gs off the flip."

"Sounds good, but I'm already flippin' work for Don."

"Yeah, so I heard." Heavy eyed Trip narrowly. "Thing is I'm tryna put you on, while Don is only tryna put himself on in this game. With the numbers, your trap spot doin', you can continue to move the light weight Don's hittin' you with and move my weight on the side. But once you're done with Don's latest load, then I want you to cut his ass off," he expounded.

"Then I'll have Don lookin' to smoke my ass if he finds out I'm workin' for you."

Swindle scoffed. "And if you don't work for us, you'll have to look out for me smokin' your ass. So, you can either get money with us and have our protection against Don and his crew, or you can look over your shoulder for me," he laid out.

"Those are your only options, Trip," Heavy added. He exhaled a thick cloud of weed smoke.

Coop piped in, "Hol' up. Y'all can't just—"

"We can, and we will," Swindle stated, cutting Coop's words short and leveled the Tec .9 on him.

Trip knew it was best to work with Heavy n'em. Not only because he didn't want to have to look over his shoulder for Swindle but also because Heavy was offering him a chance to really get his money up. He figured he'd be better off if he cutoff Don. But what he failed to realize was Don had his best interest at heart, unlike Heavy.

"A'ight. I'll move work for you," Trip agreed.

"Good." Heavy looked to Swindle and said, "Hit him with a brick." Swindle went and collected the kilo then handed it over to Trip. "Just know that no matter what, I want my paper," Heavy forewarned before Trip, along with Coop, was escorted out of the spot. Swindle took a seat on the armrest of the couch. "You know if that nigga Don finds out Trip movin' work for us, then it'll be problems."

"That's the cost of doin' business." Heavy knew that Swindle was right. And at some point, he'd have to get rid of Don.

•••

Parked curbside before the Milwaukee County Jail, Rob and TJ set in the Hellcat. They were awaiting Max, who was inside visiting their apprehended comrade, Bone. Once Max stepped out of the building and entered the backseat of the whip, Rob pulled off. They were on their way with Icewear Vezzo's "Take Somethin'" playing at a lowered volume in the background.

For nearly two years, Bone had been on lockdown fighting a robbery and murder rap. He'd been caught up after a robbery that he and the others attempted went wrong. During the caper, Bone was shot by one of the intended marks, who was then riddled with bullets. Bone's DNA was found on the scene where the robbery and murder victims were found, which led to Bone's apprehension. The cops knew there had to be more than one robber judging by the murder victims being filled with four different calibers of bullets, so they tried pressing Bone, who stuck to the G code.

"So, how is he?" Rob asked.

"He's holdin' up in there," Max told him.

"I expect nothin' less from him."

"Says his lawyer has a shot at gettin' him off at trial."

Rob dipped the Hellcat around an SUV and responded, "Good thing we all pitched in and got him that lawyer then."

"What took you so damn long?"

"Had a lot to talk about with Bone," Max answered. "And if you even care to know, he's holdin' up." He observed TJ through the rearview mirror.

TJ felt himself fluster. "Yeah, well, Bone wouldn't even be in there if his ass woulda stuck to the script."

"At least he didn't snitch on us," Max objected.

"Enough about Bone for now," Rob piped in. He braked at the stoplight on 27th and Cherry Street. "We need to focus on our next lick."

"Maybe some other time. I gotta get home to Kayla," TJ said, looking at the text message on his iPhone he'd just received from his girl.

"Damn, TJ. I see Kayla all over you and shit," Rob said as he drove off once the light flipped green.

"She loves the shit outta a nigga, that's all," TJ replied.

"Lucky you." Max snorted.

TJ brushed off the comment. "Anyway. Take me to the crib," he said.

Shortly thereafter, Rob stopped in the middle of the street before TJ's place. TJ dapped up his boys before stepping out and heading for the apartment complex where his girl, Kayla, stood awaiting at the entrance. It was still difficult for Max to see them together after all. Rob pulled off down the street.

"Look, whatever it is you're holdin' against TJ, let that shit go," Rob advised.

"Easy for you to say. Dawg, just drop me off in the hood," Max said.

"Say no more."

After dropping off his boys, Rob made his way to his l'il down bitch, Trina's, place needing to ease his mind. He spun the block twice in his Hellcat while watching his rearview mirror for any tails. He then pulled to the curb before the apartment complex and parked. Before stepping out of his car, he positioned the FN handgun on his waist. Entering the complex, Rob made his way to Trina's apartment. He knocked on the door, and a moment later, she answered. Trina stood there looking good in only a crop-top and boy-shorts, showing off her ass and titties, and displayed her matching mani/pedi while barefoot.

"And what took you so long to get here?" Trina pressed, standing with her arms folded across her breast, and her weight shifted to one side. She was short with a milk chocolate hue and a curvy frame. Being a hairstylist, she regularly wore different hairstyles. And at twenty-nine, she was still trying to get her priorities straight.

"Trina, what I tell your ass about questionin' me and shit," Rob checked her. He stepped past Trina and entered the apartment as she locked the door before trailing him into the front room. "But if you must know, I stopped in the hood to cop some weed and shit." Rob pulled out an ounce of exotic weed and a box of Swisher Sweet's blunts which he tossed atop the coffee table and said, "Roll up."

Trina took a seat on the brown couch and began breaking down one of the blunts while observing Rob remove the gun and sit it on the coffee table along with several stacks of cash. Rob used her place to stash away his goods until he was ready to move it for safekeeping. Trina was aware that he got money being a jack-boy, and she even put him up on some marks. Working at a salon, she was always surrounded with bitches who boasted about most of their niggas' business without realizing they were potentially putting a mark on their backs. And Trina had no problem being Rob's Black Bonnie.

"I need you to go and grab that cash," Rob told her as he took a seat. "And remember, if even a dime is missin', then I'ma murk your ass."

"Rob, I remember just fine, so you don't have to come at me like that," Trina replied, displaying attitude. She sparked up the blunt and then took a puff before passing it to Rob.

"Lose the 'tude, shorty. And do as I tell you."

Trina headed to her bedroom while Rob sat back on the couch, smoking the blunt. She went and collected the stash of money from inside the small safe in her bedroom closet. She then returned to the front room and strutted over to Rob, then tossed the stacks on the coffee table. Kneeling in front of him, Trina tugged at Rob's Blue Bands Only jogger pants while he held the blunt to her lips as she took a puff.

"Now go ahead and get a nigga's dick right," Rob told her.

"M'kay," Trina purred.

Rob sat back puffing the weed as Trina pulled his dick out. Her soft lips found his hardened dick, and she began sucking its tip and then licked her pierced tongue up and down the shaft. Then she swirled the balls around in her mouth as she pumped his saliva-coated dick in her manicured hand.

"Suck on it right, boo." Rob palmed her head and encouraged her to deep throat his joint. Trina's lips felt so damn good on him. She chewed him hungrily, slurping and sucking. "Just like that."

"Mmmm... This dick tastes yummy, Rob," Trina said seductively while looking up into his eyes. She licked the pre-cum from the tip of his dick. Just watching her do her thang drove Rob to a nut swelling up in the tip of his dick. Trina pumped its shaft while flicking her tongue over the tip.

"Damn, you got a nigga ready!" No longer able to control himself, Rob busted a nut, and Trina lapped it up. He relaxed back on the couch and said, "Trina, that shit was the bomb."

"And it's more where that comes from." Trina straddled his lap and began planting kisses on his neck.

"Maybe some other time, boo. Right now, I gotta go and handle some business." Rob pushed her aside on the couch.

"Really? You just gonna bounce on a bitch like that, Rob?" she complained as she watched him fix his joggers.

"Stop trippin'. I'll be back."

"How about I come by your place for a change?" Trina asked hopefully.

Rob peered at her through slits and remarked, "Trina, you know better than to ask me that shit." Almost no one knew where he laid his head at just in case someone decided to put money on it.

Trina rose to her feet and stood with her hands on her curvy hips. "So, you can trust me with your money but not with where you live?" Attitude.

"Only thing I trust is this pistol and these slugs," Rob stated as he grabbed up his FN and stuffed it on his waist.

"Whatevs, Rob. Just go and handle your business."

"Trina, you just keep playin' your position. And I'll keep playin' the streets."

Rob grabbed up the stacks of cash and then headed out the front door. He made his way to his Hellcat, brought the engine to life, and then zipped down the street playing Drake's "Money in The Grave."

CHAPTER 3

Rich stood holding up the line at Popeye's while on his iPhone taking a call. It was T-Mac on the other end. Apparently, Rich was needed back at the trap spot.

As Rich turned for the exit, he bumped into a bad l'il vibe standing there in a pink Victoria's Secret jogger suit hugging her body and a pair of Air Max. He couldn't help but admire her from head to toe. She was gorgeous in the face with soft brown eyes and her eyebrows perfectly arched. Her nose was pierced with a tiny diamond nose ring, and her hair was styled into designer cornrows. She was brown-skinned with a curvaceous frame, and it was apparent to Rich that she was confident in herself.

"Um, excuse you. Now, are you gonna order or what?" she asked, her voice kind.

"My bad. Didn't mean to hold you up," Rich spoke up once finding his voice.

"You're fine."

"And so are you." Rich smiled and caused her to blush. She had to admit that the boy is fine and drippin'. Sticking out a hand, he said, "My name's Rich."

"Brittany," she offered and gently shook his hand.

"Look, how about you let me treat you to a real dinner some night?"

"As long as it's at someplace nice."

"I wouldn't take a woman like you anyplace less than," Rich assured. Remembering he had some business to tend to, he decided to exchange Instagram accounts with Brittany before going on his way without bothering to order. Outside, he stepped into his silver Acura TSX and then pulled out of the parking lot on his way to the trap spot in the hood.

When Rich pulled up to the trap, he parked his Acura at the curb and offed its engine. T-Mac hurried out from the trap and approached the passenger side of the car, then leaned into the rolled-down window opening.

"Twelve raided the spot," T-Mac reported.

"Did they arrest anyone and confiscate anything?" Rich wanted to know.

"Naw. Luckily, no one or nothin' was in the spot at the time of the raid. But now we know Twelve is on to our trap."

"Then we gotta shutdown this trap until shit blows over."

"Rich, you know Don ain't gonna be with that shit. Especially with Heavy's trap still doin' numbers."

Rich scoffed. "In between the differences with Don and the beef with Heavy, it's a lot for one nigga to deal with."

"Listen, you and Don need to set your pride aside and have a heart to heart. As for Heavy, a bullet can easily solve that problem. And you don't have to deal with any of this shit alone; you got me."

Rich smirked because he knew T-Mac was down for him without a doubt. "And you got me too, T-Mac. But shutdown the trap for now."

"Say no more."

Interrupting them, a smoker approached the car. "Can I get a dime?" she begged of T-Mac, referring to ten dollars' worth of crack.

"I'ont have any work. Now move on," T-Mac told her, sounding annoyed as he unconsciously shoved the woman away without bothering to give her a look.

The woman then ducked her head into the car and said, "How about you? Do you have..." Her words trailed off when she and Rich's eyes met, and then she abruptly stepped away.

"Yo dawg, that was Auntie Angie," T-Mac pointed out as soon as he recognized her.

Rich jumped out of the car and went after her once, recognizing she was actually his mom. "Ma, you need to stay from around here buyin' dope."

"Don't tell me what it is I need to do. I'm still your mama, Rich," Angie replied and stopped in her tracks.

"Just barely. Maybe you could say that If you woulda spent as much time being a mother as you spend gettin' high and shit."

"You don't think I already feel bad enough for not being the mother you and Don deserve. One of the reasons why I get high is to take my mind off how much you resent me. Even if I get clean today, I don't think that'll change your opinion of me. So why even bother?" Angie's voice broke as she grew emotional. It hurt her to know that she failed as a mother, and she felt like there was nothing she could do to fix it. So, she often found herself turning to getting high in order to rid herself of self-ridicule, at least for as long as the high would last.

Rich shook his damn head. "Listen, Ma. I don't care to hear your excuses. Just don't let me catch you out here buyin' dope on this block," he told her.

"But Rich—"

"You heard what I had to say," Rich said, cutting her words short.

With no further words, Angie turned on her way. Now she needed to get high more than ever before in order to take her mind off the look of disgrace that was etched on Rich's face. She really did want to be a good mother to he and Don, but she didn't seem to know what that would take.

As Rich headed back towards his whip, he noticed T-Mac and others around observing him. Everyone in the hood knew how he and Don felt about their mama smoking crack, and if Rich or Don found out that someone was supplying Angie's habit, then they would have to answer to either of her sons.

"That wasn't right, Rich. Despite what you may think, Auntie Angie loves you and Don," T-Mac told him.

"Well, I don't feel the love." Rich stepped back into his whip and then dispersed down the street with Boosie's "Motherless Child" playing in the background. If his mother did love him and Don like Tay-Mac had said she does, then he himself didn't feel it. But Don's words echoed in his head. *At least she loves us. The streets love none.*

•••

Knowing that she couldn't go to either of her sons for some crack, Angie would get it elsewhere. Approaching the trap house, she made her way up the front porch steps and rapped on the door. A moment later, the door was pulled open by Swindle. This was one of a few trap houses he and Heavy ran throughout the hood.

Swindle was familiar with Angie because she was a regular at the trap. Sometimes he would even dope-date her, and she didn't mind being compensated for sex with crack. Like most everyone in the hood, Swindle knew she was Don and Rich's mom, and he also knew they didn't want anyone supplying her habit. But Swindle didn't give a fuck, so he'd been servin' Angie crack for a while behind Don and Rich's backs. And what made matters even worse was that they were rival dealers.

Angie's drug addiction had destroyed her life in so many different ways; she was without a house and car, no job, and most notably, it had caused a wedge between her and her sons. Rich more than Don. Angie really did want more for herself, and she wanted to get clean and get her life together. She also wanted to mend the relationship with her sons. But it was hard for any addict to get sober without help, so she found it easier to just get high and forget all about life's problems.

And even though she was on crack, Angie was still a nice-looking woman. Her skin was sandy brown, hair short, body was curvy but could be better with some weight on her, and if she wasn't as unkempt, most wouldn't be able to tell she was a crackhead. However, one day she would get herself all cleaned up. But today, Angie was chasing her very first high and would do nearly anything for it.

"Come on in," Swindle instructed and stepped aside for her to enter. He looked up and down the block to make sure no one saw Angie there before closing the door behind her. "Thought I told your ass to use the back door whenever you come to see me. We both know your sons don't want nobody servin' you around here."

"Look, whatever I do isn't their business," Angie stressed. "Now, are you gonna serve me or what?"

"Cool. What you tryna cop?"

Angie dug into the pocket of her dingy jeans and came out with eight dollars. "All I have is this here. Will you gimme a rock for it?"

"Hell, am I gonna do with that when I only serve dub rocks? Look, come up with at least double what you have there, and then I'll give you a rock."

"Swindle, please. I'll do anything for a rock. How 'bout you lemme suck your dick really good for one?" Angie practically begged.

Swindle smirked. "A'ight. But if it isn't really good like you guaranteed, then I ain't payin' you shit."

With no hesitation, Angie dropped onto her knees, then pulled Swindle's dick out of his Balmain jeans and began to suck it to hardness. She jacked his shaft in one hand while slobbering all over the tip. Once Swindle grew erect, then Angie began sucking his dick really good like she guaranteed him. He looked down at her as she sucked every inch of his joint into her warm mouth and gripped at it with her lips.

"Shit Angie, your ass definitely doin' a real good job on a nigga," Swindle grunted. He palmed the back of her skull and face-fucked her, and she took the dick into her mouth all the way down to his balls without gagging. The sounds of her moans and slurps made him bust a nut in her mouth. "Damn, that shit was bomb!"

Angie rose to her feet, wiping the slobber from around her mouth. She was always ashamed to do certain things to supply her habit, although she needed to get high badly. And Swindle knew he could use her addiction to his advantage to get what he wanted from her. He shamelessly played on her habit, and he didn't give a fuck if Don or Rich found out about how he'd mistreat their mom. If you asked him, unlike others, including Heavy, he wasn't afraid of the repercussions.

Swindle gave Angie the crack-rock she earned. "Why don't you smoke it here? 'Cause, there's much more where that comes from, as long as you'll do what I tell you."

"Anything." Angie sat on the couch and began to stuff her crack pipe with the rock. She set flames to the pipe and deeply inhaled the crack smoke.

CHAPTER 4

In the hair salon, Shanta, Parker, and Kat were seated side by side in stylists' chairs. The girls had been besties since high school, and they loved each other like sisters. It was routine for them to go and have their hair done. And the salon was where all bitches went to vent, gossip, and/or brag. Particularly about men. And Shanta and her homegirls were no different in that regard.

"Girl, I'm ready to settle down and have a family with Don, but his ass is stuck in the streets," Shanta vented. She was Don's girlfriend of three years, and their relationship was great. At twenty-eight, Shanta was a social worker and had no kids. Slim-thick with long hair, light skin, and brown eyes, she was a pretty girl. But she wasn't conceited.

"If you want to settle down, then maybe you should have a talk with Don," Parker suggested. She was a cute girl holding a petite frame, sandy brown skin with her hair dyed blond and cut stylishly short. Only twenty-seven, Parker was the manager at McDonald's and a single mom. She wanted more in life.

"Please. Niggas don't be ready to settle down until the time is right for them," Kat input. She was thirty and still trying to get her priorities straight. The type to use her good looks to get what she wanted. Kat was the hue of mahogany with natural hazel eyes. Her ass and titties were enormously enhanced, which went well with her larger-than-life attitude. "I ain't thinking about having a family right now until I find the right nigga."

"You're too busy being a slut to find the right nigga, Kat," Shanta piped in. "And what about you, Parker? Have you found Mr. Right yet?"

Parker sighed. "Girl, it's hard to find the right nigga in these streets. I need a nigga who's going to love me and hold me down."

"Unh-unh bitch. What you need is a nigga who's going to fuck you and beat it up," Kat jabbed.

"Whatevs, Kat. Anyways. Shan, are you going to have that talk with Don?"

"Don has a lot going on with his mama right now, so I don't want to bother him with my wants. Not to mention he hasn't been getting along with Rich. I'll talk with him when the time's right," Shanta said. She was becoming concerned with Don. In between him stressing over his mom, bumping heads with his brother, and striving in the streets, it seemed like as of lately, he'd been very callous. Shanta wanted Don to understand that she was there for him.

Kat's iPhone rung. She noticed it was one of her many niggas calling via FaceTime and said, "Niggas always keeping tabs on this pussy and shit."

"Good luck with that," Parker chuckled.

Shanta shook her head. "Both of you need a man."

While the girls talked among themselves, Trina over-heard them. She was familiar with them from coming in to have their hair done. They weren't exactly her friends, more so her clients. Actually, Trina was normally a hairstylist who did either of their hair. Little did the girls know, she was as dangerous as a hair-trigger.

•••

On the way to check in on one of the trap houses in the hood, Don pushed the Maxima. He and his gang now had most of the hood on lock. And though they were making good money, he knew there was always more to be made.

With a connect like Castle, all Don and his crew needed to do was expand their operation. But first thing first, they had to begin with operating their own hood, and only Heavy was standing in the way. Don planned to eventually takeover not only the hood but the city by any means.

As Don drove down the block, he noticed his mother, whom he hadn't seen in weeks. She looked disheveled, unkempt, and dirty. Angie was buying dope from Swindle, and if Don wasn't gonna feed her habit, then he damn sure wouldn't allow anyone else to. He sharply veered the Maxima to the curb, then hopped out, approaching Angie and Swindle in a temper.

"Ma, what're you doin' out here like this? Thought you were tryna get cleaned up," Don said disapprovingly. He then seized the crack rocks from her grasp.

"Don't be upset with me, Don. I'm trying," Angie replied, sounding embarrassed.

"Look, Ma. Why don't you go and get in the car?" Don ushered her to the Maxima and helped her into the passenger seat. He then turned his attention to Swindle. "From now on, don't let me find out you supplyin' my O.G. again."

Swindle held his composure. "You know how the game goes: supply and demand. Don't hate the player; hate the game," he declared.

"Don't let that be the reason I take you outta the game," Don forewarned. He then tossed the crack rocks at Swindle's feet before turning for the Maxima.

Swindle had a major dislike for Don and knew it would come a time that he was to be whacked. Had it not been for Heavy preventing him from doing so, then Swindle would have dealt with Don a long time ago. *Nigga was gon' get his*, Swindle thought, seething as he watched the Maxima pull away.

Angie couldn't even find the confidence to look at Don, so instead, she just looked out the passenger side window at the passing traffic. She hated that she let crack control her. She really did want to get cleaned up, but it wasn't so easy for her to do so. However, Don was more than willing to do what he could to help his mother beat her addiction. For as long as he could remember, she'd been a crack addict, and he wanted that to change. He wanted better for his mom for the sake of himself and Rich.

"Don," Angie began in a voice close to a whisper. "I hate that you and Rich have to see me like this. Believe me. I really do want to get clean."

"Then why do you continue to get high, Ma?" Don wanted to know.

Angie shifted towards him in her seat and said, "It's not so damn easy to just quit. I need help, baby." Tears began to sail down her cheeks.

Don pulled the car to a stop at a stoplight. "Then I'll help you. I think it's best that you go to rehab. But you gotta want it for yourself."

"Okay. I'll go to rehab if you think it'll help me. I just want to get cleaned. But what am I going to do with myself afterwards? I don't have a job or a home or anything."

"First, just worry about gettin' cleaned up. I'll make sure you're taken care of."

"Really, Donte, you'd do that for me?"

"Ma, I'd do anything for you. But you gotta promise me that you'll get clean."

"Promise. Hopefully, once I'm finally cleaned up, then Rich won't resent me as much anymore. I really want him to forgive me for not being there," Angie expressed.

"I'm sure once he sees that you're clean, he'll have a change of heart. For now, just focus on yourself, Ma," Don told her. He could only hope that Rich would admire her getting clean.

"Thank you for being here for me, baby."

"I got you." Don leaned over and pecked Angie's forehead. He loved his mother more than she knew. And like most dope boys, Don dreamt of moving his mother out of the hood.

•••

After leaving the salon, Shanta and her girls stopped by her and Don's apartment. They were getting ready for a girls' night out.

There was a knock at the front door, and Shanta answered, finding Rich on the doorstep. "Hey, Rich. Come in," she said and stepped aside, allowing him into the apartment. Upon entering the front room, Parker and Kat were seated on the chocolate brown leather couch. As Shanta sat on the chaise, she asked, "What brings you by?"

"Need to rap with Don," Rich answered.

"Well, he isn't in right now. Just me and my girls are here. But you're welcome to stay."

"Yeah, Rich, why don't you stay and smoke with us?" Kat suggested as she rolled a blunt. Shanta knew how bad Kat wanted Rich, even though Don didn't like the idea of that.

"Maybe some other time. I got shit to tend to," Rich told her.

Kat rose to her bare pedicured feet and stepped up on Rich. "Boy, why you acting like that? You know you want me, Rich."

"Kat, as bad as you are, you aren't my type. Not even if you had your shit together would I want you," Rich clowned her. He turned to Shanta. "Let Don know I dropped by."

Parker busts out laughing once Rich departed the apartment. "Girl, he told you like it is," she commented.

"Whatevs. Every nigga wants me. Rich don't know what he's missing," Kat said.

Shanta grabbed the blunt from Kat and lit it up, and told her: "Bitch, get over yourself."

After a while of kickin' it, the girls decided to go out for a bite to eat. As they were exiting the complex, Shanta noticed Don parking beside her white Nissan Altima.

"You two can wait for me in the car. I need to speak with my man real quick," Shanta told her girls.

"Hopefully, it's about what we talked about at the salon," Kat commented.

"Kat, maybe if you had a man of your own, you wouldn't be so worried over what I talk to mine about."

Parker chuckled, "She got you there."

"Whatevs," Kat remarked and flipped her hand dismissively. She stepped into the passenger seat while Parker took up the back. As Don stepped out from his whip, Shanta approached him and pecked his lips. He smirked, and half-jokingly said, "Who you lookin' good for, boo?"

"Myself. You like?" Shanta modeled in her silk Burberry blouse, which was unbuttoned just enough to reveal her cleavage that went with black fitted leather pants, which hugged her hips, thighs, and ass. She set it off with a pair of black pumps and the Burberry handbag rounding out her attire.

"No, I love it." Don admired his girl while grabbing his crotch suggestively.

"In that case, I'll look even better for you later when I'm ass naked," she replied, wearing a sultry smile.

Don pulled her close to him. "Why I gotta wait until later when we can go back inside now?"

42

"As good as that sounds, me and my girls are finna go out for drinks. So, it'll have to be later."

"Make sure your ass don't stay out too late."

"I won't. That's how I feel whenever you're out in the streets." She knew this wasn't the best time to have this discussion, but she couldn't help herself.

Don stood up straight, causing her to back up off him. "Shan, we ain't about to get into what I do in the streets."

"I'll let it go for now, only because I gotta get going with my girls."

"Good. 'Cause I get enough of that shit from my brotha."

"He stopped by not too long ago looking for you. Wanted me to let you know."

"He and I really need to talk anyway."

Shanta could read that something was bothering him. She placed a hand on his arm and said, "What is it, Don?"

"It's my ma." He leaned back up against the car and let out a sigh.

"Is she okay?" She knew how much he loved his mom after all.

Don nodded. "Don't worry. I'll take care of her. Just go and have a good time with your girls for the night. And remember to make sure you don't stay out late."

"And you make sure you wait up for me."

"Fa sho."

Don walked Shanta over to her car, where he pulled open the driver's door for her. She pecked his lips before entering the car. While he watched, Shanta, along with her girls, drove off down the street. He then pulled out his iPhone as he headed for the apartment complex. As he made his way up to his apartment, he called Rich via FaceTime. Don wondered why Rich had stopped by looking for him earlier. He figured it had to do with their street affairs. He wanted to talk with Rich about their mom. Just as Don entered the apartment, Rich answered and appeared on the screen. By his background, Don could see that Rich was with Tay-Mac sitting in his whip smoking weed.

"Shan told me you stopped by lookin' for me," Don said. He closed the front door and made his way over to the couch in the front room, where he took a seat. "What was that about?"

"About you reopenin' the trap after I shut it down," Rich answered. He puffed on the blunt.

"Look, I get that you wanted the trap shut down for a while because of Twelve, but we stand to lose out on movin' product that way. I ain't with allowin' Heavy and his boys gaining our clientele and profits."

"Don, you need to make sure you talk with Heavy ASAP, so we don't have to be in any competition with him and his boys. Because if not, then we stand to lose out due to beef."

"I'ma talk with Heavy as soon as I get the chance. And if he wants beef, then I'ma gibe it to 'em," Don stated.

"Then so be it," Rich replied. No matter his much he didn't agree with how his big bro did shit, he was always ready and willing to ride or die for Don.

"Now that's out the way, while I got you on the phone, I wanna talk with you about our mom."

"And why should I care about her, Don?"

"'Cause, Rich, she needs you too. And if you care to know, I just took her to a rehab center."

Rich scoffed. "And?"

"And she needs our support. Can't you see that moms is tryin' to get clean? Isn't that what you want?"

"No, that's what you want. What I want is to let her be."

Don shook his damn head. "You don't mean that shit, Rich. And once she's finally clean, I hope you be there for

her as much as I'll be. I'ma buy her a home and move her out
the hood. She deserves a chance."

"I'll tell you what. If moms gets clean, then I'll think
about givin' her a chance," Rich said. "Look, I got some shit
I need to tend to. How about you meet me at the trap
sometime tomorrow so we can discuss some business?"

"I'll be there. Bro, just know that our business don't have
to get so personal."

After ending the call with his l'il bro, Don leaned back in
his seat with a lot on his mind. He knew he had to remain
focused on making sure he and his gang continue to get their
money and weight up. However, he understood that he had
to make Heavy see shit his way, or there was bound to be
bloodshed. And blood on the money was bad for business.
Then there was shit with his moms. Helping her get clean
would be a task, especially since Rich wasn't willing to be of
much help due to his resentment towards her. Don hoped that
he and his l'il bro could get past their differences because he
loved Rich no matter what. Shanta and her concerns shifted
through his mind. He didn't want her to be concerned with
his street life being that it was the lifestyle that had chosen
him.

Minus the bullshit, life's great, Don mused.

Martell "Troublesome" Bolden

CHAPTER 5

The gamble spot was crowded. Some niggas were placing bets on all sorts of games, while others were huddled in corners plotting on how they'd get their losses back. The spot attracted major ballers from throughout the streets, so there was always major cash coming in and going out of the place. And the spot was guarded, there were security cameras installed on the inside and outside of the house, and not to mention there were armed niggas securing the place. Thus far, the house had no problems as money was won and lost.

Don stood beside Heavy at a pool table with C-Note and Swindle hanging close by. The two had agreed to meet at the spot without their crews, aside from their right-hand-men, in order to discuss business. Don was out to convince Heavy to see things his way. He knew that with him and Heavy competing to supply their hood, it was bound to turn into a war over money, power, and respect.

"Heavy, the thing here is we're both gettin' too big for one hood. So, the only way I see shit working out is if one of us supplies the other," Don was saying.

"And I take it you just expect for me to cop supply from you, so you can have the hood on lock," Heavy replied.

"You takin' it the wrong way. This isn't about me tryna lockdown the hood. Look, I got a major plug on deck, and I can flood you at will. So, all I'm sayin' is with my plug and your clientele, we both stand to get money in the hood without bein' competitors."

"Don, all I hear you sayin' is if shit don't go your way, then it's beef. Well, I'ont beef unless I need to. That said, I'll continue to get money without you and your plug."

"Shit don't have to be that way. What I'm tryna do is get money with you," Don stressed.

Heavy snorted. "Seems to me that what you're tryna do is get more money than me. Always remember that with the more money you come across, the more problems you'll see."

"Well, you remember this, I haven't run from a problem yet." Don left Heavy with that thought as he turned and headed out the gamble spot with C-Note in tow.

Heavy noticed Swindle start to trail behind them and asked, "Hell you goin'?"

"Finna go and air out the nigga Don. Ain't gonna let him get the chance to come for us first," Swindle told him.

"Won't be necessary. Don's not comin' for us because he isn't tryna start any beefs. The nigga knows there will be too much bloodshed and money lost that way."

"Heavy, what that nigga knows is that if he offs you, then he'll be able to supply the whole hood and make more money. It's what he wants anyway. The only reason he offered to flood you is to keep you under him. But since you turned down his offer, now I'm sure Don won't mind puttin' you under the dirt," Swindle expounded.

Heavy leaned down to take a shot on the pool table. "Just be easy for now. If Don tries somethin', then we'll get at his ass," he instructed. Once Heavy took his shot, he scratched. "Shit."

It bothered Swindle that Heavy was sleeping on the nigga Don. He was sure the nigga would try to move on Heavy, but not if he had something to do about it beforehand. "Luckily, Heavy have me around to do the dirty work," Swindle said, introspectively.

Outside, Don and C-Note headed towards Don's Maxima that was parked curbside. The discussion with Heavy was still on Don's mental. He wasn't at all surprised that Heavy had declined his proposal. In fact, he more so expected it. Don just hoped to avoid a possible drug beef in the hood.

"Now that Heavy denied doin' business with us, what's our next move?" C-Note wanted to know.

"We take Heavy's clientele and bleed his operation dry by offerin' better prices and quality of work. That way, he'll either have to cop from us or have to leave the hood," Don explained.

"And what if he wants to beef with us over the hood?"

"The hood isn't big enough for the both of us."

Don stepped into the Maxima, and C-Note followed. They set off on their way.

•••

"You niggas ready?" Rob asked his comrades as he pulled down his ski mask over his face and then checked the slide of his FN handgun.

"Let's do this," Max said, gripping tightly on his Glock .26 in his lap.

"We get in, and we get out," TJ told them. He made sure his Mac-11 was ready for action.

The three set in the Lex' truck parked outside of the gamble house. Tonight, they'd be running in the spot and laying it down. After observing the house for the past three nights, They each had also been inside of the house, so they knew its layout. They were all masked up, strapped, and ready to murk a nigga if need be. In the dead of the night, the trio hopped outta the SUV and insidiously made their way up the porch steps to the front door of the gamble house. Rob forcefully kicked open the door and quickly stepped aside, allowing Max and then TJ to raid the house ahead of him. Max immediately disarmed the nigga of his A.R.-15, who stood on guard at the front door before he could even process what was taking place. Max tucked his Glock into his waistband and leveled the confiscated A.R.-15 on the house full of gamblers, while Rob and TJ were on ten.

Boc! Boc! Boc!

Rob shot into the ceiling thrice, commanding everyone's undivided attention, and then shouted, "Nobody moves, nobody gets murked!" He brandished his FN.

Rob was flanked by Max and TJ as they swept their weapons around the room. All three of the jack boys' eyes darted from one gambler to the next, seeking for the first nigga that didn't want to comply with the demands made. Max stood back up against the wall beside the front door to keep everyone in his sight while on guard, leveling the confiscated A.R.-15. After Rob and TJ were confident that everyone would follow their orders, they began to move through the room and confiscate anything of value: money, jewelry, and drugs, which were all tossed into the backpack they carried along.

Rob approached a nigga standing near a pool table and ripped a stack of cash from his grip, who was Swindle. While seizing the paper, the iced-out chain around Swindle's neck caught Rob's eye, and he firmly hissed, "Nigga, take it off!"

"Listen, bro—"

Thump!

Swindle's words were cut short once Rob slammed his FN upside his head before pressing its barrel to the nigga's temple. Rob firmly stated, "It wasn't a suggestion."

Swindle began removing the chain hurriedly as blood dripped onto its diamonds from the laceration on his head which Rob's gun had just caused due to the vicious strike. After seizing the chain, Rob and TJ continued their collection. Max, who remained standing near the front door, heard someone walking up the front porch steps. After there was a rap on the door, Max yanked it open and pointed the A.R.-15 at the two niggas standing outside on the porch, causing them to jump back in shock.

"Get the fuck in here," Max ordered while stepping aside, allowing space for them to enter. Max forced the niggas facedown onto the floor and then stepped back near the door, allowing TJ to also gather their belongings.

"Everyone lay face down on the floor. Now!" TJ directed the gamblers after he and his boys had gathered everything they had come for.

Max pulled open the door letting Rob and TJ walk out ahead of him, and then he began backing out of the door with his A.R.-15 raised before spinning on his heels and sprinting to the SUV behind his comrades. They peeled off down the street.

Martell "Troublesome" Bolden

CHAPTER 6

"We gotta do somethin' about this nigga. Can't let shit like this slide."

Don had concerns about a nigga in his gang, Trip, going against the grain. He was told that Trip had been servin' work on the side for another plug, and Don wasn't having that shit. The way Don saw it was there was money being taken from the pockets of him and his gang. And ain't no nigga taking from him or his without there being repercussions.

Sitting in the new cocaine-white Range Rover he'd recently purchased, Don was parked in the hood with Danger in the passenger seat. It was just barely afternoon, and the hood was live with pack-boys servin' smokers. It wasn't shit for each of the pack-boys to get off their packs by evening.

Don looked to Danger and said, "I need you to find out who Trip been movin' work for on the side. As for Trip, that nigga dead to me."

"And I'ma make sure of that," Danger assured.

•••

Behind one of the trap houses, C-Note parked the gray Dodge Magnum in the dark back alley. He was with Danger, and they were there to see one of the top pushers, Trip. Entering the spot, they found Trip there alone, seated on the couch in the front room, counting up the day's profits at the coffee table.

"Apparently you doin' numbers," C-Note said, seeing the numerous stacks of cash. He took a seat on the arm of the couch while Danger remained standing.

"Numbers don't lie," Trip responded with a grin. "This is close to sixty bands. Woulda been more, but I ran outta work and had to shut down the trap for the night. You bring more work?"

"No, I'm just here to pick up the bread. Besides, you won't be needin' anymore."

Trip looked at him perplexed. "What you mean?"

"I mean, we're no longer in need of your services."

Trip then felt a barrel pressed to the back of his skull, and before he knew it, Danger pulled the trigger.

Blam!

The .40 caliber bullet blew through Trip's head, splattering blood on the money. While C-Note tossed the cash into a pillowcase, Danger rolled up the corpse inside the throw rug on the floor. They carried the body rolled up inside the rug out the back door of the spot and unceremoniously dumped it in the alley. Afterward, C-Note and Danger hopped into the Magnum and set off to let Don know that Trip was a dead deal.

•••

"You sure Don is the one who killed Trip?" Heavy asked.

"Who else?" Swindle answered the question with a question.

They were in their trap spot. Once Swindle had gone looking to make a pickup/drop-off and found Trip, who'd been dead for a couple of days from a bullet to the head, Swindle immediately knew that Don had something to do with it. Because Swindle had been the one to make sure Don found out Trip was pushing work for Heavy on the side. Afterward, Swindle rushed to Heavy and broke the news with the effort to give Heavy the idea to take Don out.

"Think about it," Swindle went on, "Trip was movin' work for you on the side, and somehow Don must've found out. Don killed him in order to send you a message. Not to mention he took all of your profit and product to add insult to injury."

Heavy leaned back in his seat and caressed his chin. "Sounds about right. Don got shit twisted if he thinks I ain't on to him."

"And now you need to send Don a message in return," Swindle pressed. He was standing near the front door.

"You know what, you're right. Grab a couple of shooters, and y'all spin on that nigga Don," Heavy directed.

"Say less."

Little did Heavy know, Swindle already had two shooters on standby. He'd anticipated encouraging Heavy to give him the greenlight to go at Don. Call it manipulation, but the way Swindle saw it was that he just needed to offer Heavy a little nudge to do what was in their best interest by having Don smoked one way or another.

Martell "Troublesome" Bolden

CHAPTER 7

Rob pulled his Hellcat into the parking lot of his apartment complex and parked. He was returning home after leaving Trina's place. Departing from the car, he closed the door, chirped the alarm, and then headed towards the building. Before Rob knew it, a dark figure approached, and Rob reached for the FN on his waist. He halted, once realizing who it was.

"Bone?" Rob said soberly. He was surprised to see his past comrade.

"Don't look so damn surprised, Rob," Bone responded. He was dark skin with an athletic build and low cut. Not one to back down from no one, Bone faced whoever with intent to kill.

Rob removed his hand from the butt of his gun and said, "Nigga, I almost popped your ass, showin' up unannounced." Flustered.

"Difference between you and me, I woulda popped off," Bone declared.

Rob smirked. "Still the same, I see."

"Ain't shit change. Unfortunately, jail doesn't seem to offer rehabilitation."

"Yeah. Well, fortunately, you're finally outta jail. But how?"

"No gun, no case," Bone simply put. He had walked free after trial due to there being a lack of substantial evidence to convict him of the robbery and murder charges.

"It took longer than expected."

"Nearly three years in jail is a long time. Definitely, when nobody's lookin' out for you after all you've done for them."

"Bone, it wasn't even like that."

Bone scoffed. "It was straight like that. Where were y'all when I needed help? The lawyer and commissary didn't pay itself."

"Look, Bone, it was best for all of us the less we were in contact once you went down in order to keep the heat off of us," Rob reasoned.

"I went down for all of you and took a bullet in the process, Rob. Y'all owe me, dammit!" Bone retorted.

"So, what is it you want? Huh?"

"For starters, I want my cut of the fuckin' money from the lick I went down for. Or I want back in on any other licks lined up."

"That's somethin' we'll have to work out."

"Work out? I coulda worked out a deal with the D.A., but I chose to keep quiet instead," Bone remarked. "Look, I'll meet with you and the gang at the usual pool hall later tonight. Then we'll work things out there." He turned on his way.

Rob understood why Bone felt like he had turned his back on him. He wasn't worried about Bone being a back-stabber because he knew Bone was a cutthroat. Therefore, he would be sure to keep Bone close. And Rob expected that Bone would return, wanting the money owed to him from the lick. He understood that money determines loyalty, and loyalty could cost others their lives.

•••

In the pool hall, Rob, TJ, and Max occupied a booth. After Bone had shown up at Rob's place earlier, he needed to meet up with the others to discuss how they should go about dealing with Bone. Even though Bone had taken the fall for them, it was Bone's own damn fault the cops had gotten onto them in the first place. However, Bone did show and proved his loyalty by not mentioning any names when he had gotten jammed. However, each of them held individual feelings towards Bone.

Rob sipped from his glass of Hennessey while they were awaiting Bone's arrival. "If you ask me, we don't even owe Bone an explanation. He's the reason why everything went bad three years ago," he was saying.

"Agreed," TJ second.

"But he didn't snitch on us. Doesn't that mean somethin'?" Max piped in in Bone's defense.

"Means that we can trust him," Rob admitted.

TJ scoffed. "I'ont trust the nigga much at all. We don't know if he has ill will after havin' to sit in jail for so long. Nigga could be out to make us pay."

"Only thing we'll pay is what he's owed from the last lick he was in on. That's it."

"And what about him wantin' in on other licks we have lined up?" TJ asked.

Rob sat his drink on the table. "I take it you don't want him back in with us on hittin' licks."

"I'ont think it's a good idea given what happened the last time we were on a lick with Bone."

"And why not, TJ? Don't forget that he was part of our gang before," Max objected.

"And don't you forget that he almost got our gang knocked." TJ's tone was hostile.

"But he took the rap so the rest of the gang wouldn't have to," Max retorted.

Rob piped in, "Let's just meet with Bone first before we determine anything. A'ight?"

As if on cue, Bone entered the pool hall, and as he approached them, the gang grew silent. Making himself comfortable, Bone took a seat in the booth beside Rob, helped himself to Rob's glass of Hennessey, and turned it up to his lips.

"Been a long time since we were all here together like this," Bone said, relatively calm.

"Time flies," Rob replied.

"Unless you're stuck in a cell doin' time," Bone remarked.

"Yeah, well, a cell is better than a grave," TJ input.

Bone snorted and then took a swig of the liquor. "Only difference between the two is the possibility of freedom."

"And it's good to see you're finally free," Max said.

"Fa sho. And Max, good lookin' for bein' the only one to pay me a visit while I had to be on lockdown." Bone shifted in his seat, getting a better look at the gang, and said, "Speakin' of payin' me, I expect my cut from our last lick. All sixty G's of it."

"Well, don't expect for us to have it for you right now," Rob told him.

"Then I expect for you to get it for me right away. Or how about I get back in on hittin' licks, and we call it even?" Bone suggested.

"And why should we trust you back with the gang, Bone?" TJ wanted to know.

"Because I have never given you a reason to distrust me."

"Besides, he's originally part of this gang," Max added.

Rob leaned back in his seat. "And I started this gang. Bone, you can get back to hittin' licks with us. But shit will go my way, so I won't have none of that shit you pulled that almost got us all knocked," he declared.

"Whatever you say, Rob. Just let me know when's the next lick," Bone said.

Money in the Grave

Approaching the booth with a glass of Rémy on rocks in hand, Kayla handed the drink over to TJ and then pecked him on the lips. She almost didn't recognize Bone.

Bone looked to Kayla and smirked. "Still look as good as the last time I saw you."

TJ rose from the booth, placing a hand on the small of Kayla's back, and said, "Give us a minute, will you." Once she stepped away, he then returned his attention to Bone. "You feelin' some type of way?"

"No hard feelings." Bone drowned the remains of the drink, then stood from the booth and said, "Good lookin' for the drink, Rob. Max, I'll be in touch. And TJ, give Kay my best... if you can." He turned on his way and headed out of the pool hall.

TJ knew now that Bone was out of jail; it could spell trouble. Nearly three years ago, they'd hit a lick that went wrong, and Bone had taken the heat with the understanding that he'd return to his share of the take. And now Bone was out for his and more.

"What the hell were you thinkin', Rob?" TJ wanted to know heatedly. He plopped down back in his seat.

"I'm thinkin' we can use Bone to pull off bigger capers," Rob replied evenly.

"And I'm with Rob on this," Max input.

"Don't you two realize that Bone is tryna get over on us." TJ shook his damn head.

Rob looked dead into TJ's eyes and swore, "The only way Bone will do so is over my dead body."

•••

During the ride home with Kayla, TJ drove in silence. From time to time, he would glance over at Kayla, and she

61

would smile at him. TJ did actually make Kayla happy, and she wanted a future with him. However, it didn't take away from the fact that she did have a past with Bone. Before Bone had gone to jail, though he and Kayla had only been together only a few months, they shared something that at the time was good. But Kayla had turned to TJ for comfort in the absence of Bone, and she and TJ unintentionally developed mutual feelings. Then once Kayla decided she wanted to be with TJ, she at least had the decency to go and visit with Bone one last time and tell him the truth. Now all Kayla wanted was to be happily in love with TJ, while Bone couldn't care less about their love and happiness.

Once they arrived at their apartment complex, TJ parked his black Audi truck in the parking lot. The two stepped out the whip and entered the complex. Inside the apartment, TJ made his way into the bedroom, where Kayla was seated before the vanity mirror, removing her jewelry. TJ placed his pole on the nightstand, then stepped up behind Kayla and caressed her shoulders. "What did Bone want?" Kayla inquired, placing her three-karat diamond earrings inside a jewelry box.

"It's nothin'." TJ sighed sharply.

She peered up at him over her shoulder and replied, "Must be something for him to show up there after all this time. Is everything okay?"

"Don't worry. I'll handle it."

"I just don't want there to be any bad blood between you and him over me."

"This has nothin' to do with you, Kayla. Look, Bone had his chance with you, but you're with me now. And we're happy together, right?"

Kayla nodded. "Right."

Money in the Grave

TJ planted kisses on Kayla's neck. He pulled her onto her feet and began helping her out of her body-hugging Versace dress. She then returned the favor and helped him out of his attire. The two stood before the mirror, admiring how good they looked together. TJ, with his slim build, towered over a slim-thick Kayla, and their good looks complimented each other. Raising on her tiptoes, Kayla pulled TJ's mouth onto hers, and they engaged in a passionate kiss. Their tongues caressed one another as their hands explored each other's bodies. His dick was stiff and her pussy moist.

TJ bent Kayla over the vanity dresser and slid down her black lace thong, and she stepped out of it. He then pulled off his Polo boxer briefs. While holding her ass steady, he guided his joint into her slit from behind. As each inch of the dick filled Kayla's pussy, she set free a pleasurable moan. TJ loved the feeling of her wetness as his pipe slipped back and forth in her slit. He stared into her eyes through their reflection in the mirror.

"Who pussy is this, huh? Whose is it?" TJ wanted to know as he fucked Kayla like never before.

"It's yours, TJ! This pussy is yours!" Kayla purred. She arched her back, giving TJ more access to her pussy. Gripping her ass, TJ dug her out and hit her spot. Kayla tossed her head back with her mouth agape and eyes closed shut as she felt an orgasm teasing her. "Shit... I'm cummmin!"

Kayla turned around and hungrily kissed TJ as she ushered him backwards to the king-size bed. She pushed him back onto the bed, then climbed atop him and began rocking her slick pussy back and forth on his stiff dick. TJ held Kayla at the waist, and she dug her manicure into his bare chest while she rode him. He enjoyed the feel of her wetness gripping at his hardness.

"Damn, this wet got a nigga ready to bust, boo!" TJ grunted as he felt a nut swell in the tip of his dick. Kayla bounced on his lap until he exploded.

After their quickie, TJ lay in bed beside Kayla. He couldn't help but wonder how Bone must've felt seeing him with her. It wasn't like I intentionally tried to get with Kayla; it just happened, he contemplated. Now she's mine, and Bone will have to accept that. TJ kissed Kayla's forehead while her head rests on his bare chest. He was willing to lay down his life for her.

Now that Bone was back in the streets, TJ was sure that he was back with a vengeance.

CHAPTER 8

It had been three weeks since Angie was checked into the rehab center. The road to sobriety wasn't easy at all for her. Like with any addict, it takes lots of willpower. For the first week, Angie suffered through withdrawals which were so terrible that she even considered just giving up and leaving the center to go and get high. But she knew that she needed to complete the Twelve-step program for the sake of herself, and the thought of having Don and Rich being proud of her gave her the strength to continue. Don and Angie sat on a bench outside of the center. He made sure to come to visit her at least twice a week, not only to check on her and her progress but also to show his love and support.

"Ma, you're lookin' much better now," Don complimented his mother. He noticed Angie was well-kempt, put on some weight, and looked well-rested.

"Actually, now I feel much better," Angie replied.

"Looks like rehab is working for you."

"I'll say. I just wish that I would've done it long ago. Then maybe life would be much different for me."

Don grabbed her hand in his. "Ma, what matters most is that you're doin' it now. It's not too late for you to make a difference in life."

"But it's too late for me to make a difference in you and your brother's lives. If it wasn't for me being a bad mom, the two of you might be better off." Her tone was regretful.

"Bein' addicted to drugs doesn't make you a bad mom. All that matters is that you loved us."

"That's not what Rich thinks. Every time he looks at me, I see resentment in his eyes."

"Rich doesn't resent you, Ma."

"Then how come he hasn't been to visit since I've been here?"

Don squeezed her hand. "Look, I'll have a talk with Rich. Once you're out of here and he sees your change, then I'm sure he'll look at you differently."

"I hope so. And what about you, Don?"

"What do you mean?" Angie shifted towards him. "I mean, if I'm getting clean, then you can clean up your act also. And you're the one who can convince Rich to do so as well."

"Ma," he looked away, "this isn't about Rich or me. Just focus on yourself for now."

"Listen, baby. I just don't want anything to happen to you or your brother. I know how things go in the dope game; you'll either end up in prison or in a grave. And as much as you want me to get my life together, I want you to have a better life."

Don had to admit that she made a point. He met her eyes and said, "I can take care of myself in the game. As for Rich, I'll look after him like I always have, even when he don't care for me too. So, don't worry about him and me. Just worry about getting yourself cleaned up so you can come home."

"Okay, I will."

"I gotta get goin'. I'll be back soon." Don pecked her on the cheek before rising and heading away.

"Don," she called after him. "Tell Rich I love him."

"I'll let you tell him for yourself." Don continued on his way with Rich on his mind.

•••

66

Don drove through the streets aimlessly with a lot on his mind. He needed to talk with Rich about their mom. Knowing that his mom was hurt behind Rich resenting her was heavy on Don. On the flip side, he understood why Rich felt the way he did. But he himself was against it. Don turned the Range headed for Rich's place. They needed to have a talk that was long overdue.

Don rapped on the front door of Rich's apartment, and a moment later, Rich answered. The two held eyes, neither wavering.

"Gon' let me in, or what," Don said. Without words, Rich just turned and walked inside, leaving Don at the door, who shut the door behind himself before following his brother.

"And what brings you by?" Rich wanted to know as he sat on the couch in the front room.

"Mama wants to see you, Rich."

Rich scoffed. "Well, I'ont wanna see her."

"And why not?"

"Don, you know exactly why. She hasn't given a fuck about us ever since I could remember," he retorted.

"She was sick," Don reasoned.

"Sick? Let's just call it what it is; she's an addict."

"And she's tryna beat her addiction. All she needed was some help. And now what she needs is our support."

Rich shook his damn head. "Don't you get it? She'll never get clean if she hasn't by now."

"What if you're wrong, huh? What if she gets cleaned up after all?"

"Enough with the ifs, Don. She didn't come to see me while I was on lockdown, so why should I go and see her now? Besides, she's never been there to support us."

"So, that's what this is about; you havin' a grudge? Well, that's not good for you, Rich. She's not the one in the wrong; you are," Don declared.

Rich jumped to his feet and snapped, "What's wrong is you expect for me to just forgive mama when she doesn't deserve it. And it's obvious she loves you over me any-fuckin'-way!" He glared into his big brother's eyes.

"No, Rich, mama loves you just the same. And you love her more than you care to admit. Just remember that no matter how much she wasn't there for us growin' up, we only get one mom. Hopefully, you take that for what it's worth," Don told him. With no further words, he turned and departed the apartment leaving Rich to his thoughts.

Rich plopped back down on the couch. He had to admit that his big brother was right about him loving his mom. It just hurt him that he loved her so much, but she seemed to love getting high more than her own sons. Part of him understood it was the addiction that controlled her actions, although he didn't want to offer her any excuse.

A mom is supposed to love her kids and be there for them no matter what, Rich thought. But shouldn't the feelings be mutual? Maybe Don was right to support their mom after all. Besides, who was Rich to judge his mom when he supplied the very drug that destroyed her life.

Rich needed to ease his mind. He grabbed the half-smoked blunt from the ashtray on the end table and lit it up. *I'm sorry, mama*, he mused as he puffed the blunt. *I never meant to hurt you.*

CHAPTER 9

Seated in the VIP section of the 618 Nightclub, Don was accompanied by Shanta, along with C-Note and Danger and Kat and Parker. Courtesy of Don, they were in there doin' it big. He and the others were seated on a white leather couch with bottles on chill in a bucket of ice on their table. And in between his brand-new Range Rover parked outside and the iced-out chain around his neck, Don was flexin' with no effort. He had asked Rich to come out with them, but Rich declined, not really one to play the club scenes because he didn't like unwanted attention. Unlike Don, whose flexin' drew attention whenever he was on the scene. It was apparent that over time he and his gang had gotten their money and weight up.

"Too bad Rich and T-Mac aren't here to get lit with us. They need to chillax, especially Rich," Don said and then turned up the bottle of Ace of Spades to his lips. Then he placed the bottle to Shanta's lips who set on his lap.

"Rich is just cautious with how he moves," C-Note commented.

Danger snorted. "Too cautious if you ask me."

The three men chuckled at Rich's expense.

"Baby, me and my girls are gonna go to the restroom to freshen up," Shanta said. She pecked Don on the lips before she and Kat and Parker headed off.

"That bitch, Kat, bad! I'ma fuck around and slide to the telly with her tonight," Danger said as he checked out Kat's phat ass while she and the others headed for the restroom.

"Watch it, my nigga. That bitch ain't shit but a sack chaser," Don warned.

"And a nigga don't need a bitch like that in his life," C-Note added.

"Well, the only thing that bitch gon' get from me is some dick," Danger assured.

Don sipped at his bottle. "Enough about that bitch. I have been thinkin' about coppin' more weight. I want to expand our operation."

"Sounds good. And since we been spendin' good money with Castle, I'm sure he'll front us if we ask," C-Note said.

"What about the nigga Heavy? He's really been gettin' in the way of us makin' more paper. And since Heavy isn't willin' to cop work from us, then he isn't worth shit to us," Danger expounded.

"Then we'll just have to spin on that nigga." Don leaned back in his seat and said, "Now, let's pour up."

•••

At the pool hall, Rob and his gang were all having a night out. While Rob and TJ stood around drinking beer, Bone and Max shot a game of pool. Tonight was normal enough.

"Now that I'm back with the gang, we should put the past behind us," Bone said.

"Bone, as long as you don't repeat your past mistake, then we shouldn't have any problems in the future," Rob told him.

TJ took a swig from his bottle of Budweiser. "And if there are any problems, then the best way to solve it is to exclude you from the gang all together with no more chances."

"TJ, who are you to say what's best for any of us?" Max piped in.

"Look, I'm just sayin' that we don't need anyone part of the gang that will put us all in jeopardy."

Bone scoffed. "The problem is you didn't care to give me a chance, to begin with."

"And maybe you're right. It's not like I'ont have my reason," TJ remarked.

"Don't let Kayla be the reason, TJ," Bone retorted.

Rob decided to pipe in: "What's done is done. So, both you let it go."

Seeing the gang, Solo decided to approach them. He knew they were getting paid off hittin' licks, and he wanted in. Solo was slim with a low cut. He was a petty hustler who got in where he fit in, and more than anything, Solo was out for himself.

As Solo stepped towards the crew, he peeped Bone clutch the pole on his waist. "Be easy. I'm just here to talk business," Solo clarified.

"What business do you have with us?" Rob wanted to know. He took a swig from his beer bottle.

"And it better be good," Bone added.

"Is a lick for at least fifty bands and some dope good enough?"

"That depends," TJ said.

"Depends on what?" Solo asked.

"On what you want out of it."

"What I want is to be down with your gang, is all."

Max knocked a pool ball into the side pocket and then said, "And why should we let you be down with our gang?"

"Because I can put y'all up on other licks. Not to mention I'm one of the only niggas who know how y'all get down," Solo pitched.

Bone eyed him narrowly. "And why should we trust you?"

"Because I could hit this lick without y'all. But instead, I'm choosin' to bring y'all with me. So, if y'all down then, I'm talkin' about ridin' out tonight."

Rob knew it was best not to fuck with no new niggas, but he had an ulterior motive. Rob told him: "We're down."

"Cool. Before we ride out, lemme go and have myself a couple of shots." Solo turned and went on his way over to the bar.

"Rob, we don't need that nigga in our damn business," TJ asserted.

"Bad enough he already talks too fuckin' much," Max added.

Bone snorted. "You two just don't get it. Rob knows what he's doin'."

"Listen up. It's right that we don't need him in our business because he does talk too much. So, with him knowin' our get down, it means we just gotta play him close for now," Rob told the gang. He understood their concerns; however, money was the motive.

While Solo was standing at the bar throwing back shots, Rob made his way over, and the gang followed suit. Rob ordered another round for Solo, who was already tipsy. The barkeeper poured up yet another shot and set it atop the bar.

"This last shot is on me," Rob smirked.

•••

Shanta stood checking her beat in the mirror with her girls doing just the same on either side of her. She didn't wear much makeup being naturally pretty. Tonight, Shanta was looking cute with her hair in curls and wearing a cream-colored, form-fitting Chanel dress and red heels with a matching red clutch purse. And her girls were looking just as cute, Kat rocking a blond lace front wig and a black Gucci bodysuit with yellow open-toe stilettos, and Parker with her hair stylishly short and sporting a teal Prada romper with white pumps. They had niggas gawking and bitches gagging.

"The nigga Danger been eyeing you all night, Kat," Shan pointed out.

"Him and every other nigga in here," Kat replied as she reapplied her canary yellow lipstick.

"Danger is kinda cute though, girl," Parker added.

Kat cut her eyes at Parker then remarked, "Then bitch, why don't you holla at his ass."

"Kat, I ain't the one he's been eyeing. Besides, there's someone I'm interested in," she informed her girls.

"Well, the only nigga in here I want is Don," Shan piped in. "And I'm sure he feels the same about me."

Parker shook her head. "Not every bitch is lucky enough to be with a nigga like Don."

"True. Look, let's get back to the table before Don starts wondering where I am."

Shanta led the way out of the restroom with her home-girls in tow. As they maneuvered through the clubbers, a nigga named Tank approached Shanta, trying to get with her. She could tell he was inebriated judging by his slur and the bottle of Cîroc in his hand. He was a baldheaded nigga with a full beard and a build similar to an offensive lineman. And the nigga couldn't seem to take a hint that Shanta wasn't feeling him.

"I'm sayin' boo, you ain't gon' give a nigga your number," Tank said in a slur.

"No, I'm good," Shanta replied.

"So, it's like that?"

"What part of no don't you understand? The N or the O?" Kat sassed.

"Now, will you leave our girl alone?" Parker added.

Tank aggressively grabbed Shanta's arm as she turned to walk away and raved, "Bitch, you don't gotta act all stuck up and shit!"

From the couch over in the VIP section, Don and his boys could see the entire scene unfold.

"Yo Don, you see that fool-ass nigga all over your girl," Danger pointed out.

"Nigga must be outta his mind," C-Note commented.

"Then let's go and get his mind right," Don stated. He and his boys made a beeline over to the commotion. Don pulled Shanta behind him and then stepped to the nigga with C-Note and Danger at his flank. "If you know what's best for you, then you'll leave my bitch alone and go on your way," he warned Tank.

"Nigga you came over here to save this bitch, like I'm 'posed to be scared or some shit 'cause you and your crew runnin' it up in the game. Fuck you, your crew, and your bitch!" Tank barked.

"Watch your fuckin' mouth. And like I told you, go on your way."

As Don turned to walk away, then Tank tried taking a wild swing at him, but Don was able to see the punch coming and wove out of the way. Don countered with a blow to Tank's jaw, and then C-Note and Danger immediately helped jump the lineman-sized nigga. As the trio delivered Tank an ass beating, the club's security hurried over and broke up the brawl and then escorted Tank outside, being that he was the one who started the beef and not to mention Don was a regular there and always spent good money.

Afterwards, Don and the rest all returned to their table over in VIP. For the remainder of the night, they enjoyed themselves like nothing ever happened. Danger and Kat had gotten more acquainted and even planned to spend the night at the hotel after the club. C-Note danced with Parker on the dance floor. As for Don and Shanta, they were all over each other. She was happy to have him in her life to protect her and provide for her. Don loved being the only nigga Shanta needed in her life. She was his. As the night went on, the group poured up, danced to the music, and enjoyed each other's company.

Near closing time, the group headed out of the club. Don and Shanta made their way towards his Range, along with C-Note and Parker. Danger and Kat headed for his Donk Chevy, which were parked side by side in the parking lot. While the girls were sitting in the whips, Don, C-Note, and Danger stood outside shooting the breeze. Suddenly, Tank stepped from in between two parked cars with a gun in hand!

Blam! Blam! Blam!
Boom! Boom!

As Tank busted at Don, who ducked for cover, Danger was quick on the draw with his own pistol and busted back. The nigga Tank was struck down by a couple of fatal shots to his chest, and his big frame slammed onto the pavement. Don n'em hopped in their whips and sped out of the parking lot, leaving Tank slumped as an example that they weren't to be fucked with. And they weren't worried about no one snitching on them to Twelve out of either fear or respect. Either way, they had a lock on the streets.

•••

Knock, knock, knock
"Who dat?" a dope boy asked from inside the trap spot.

"It's me, Juicy," the crackhead announced herself. Once hearing the door being unlocked, she scurried away. She'd done the task she was paid to do.

After hearing the familiar name of a regular customer, the dope boy opened the door, and, to his dismay, he found himself staring down the barrel of an FN with a masked man behind the trigger.

Thump!

Rob slapped the FN upside the dope boy's head which forced him to topple backwards into the house and spill onto the floor. Instantly TJ, Max, Bone, and Solo rushed into the trap with their guns aimed and ready. They made three more dope boys, along with two bitches lay face down on the floor. While Max held the marks at gunpoint with an A.R.-15, Rob and TJ frisked them all, and Bone and Solo went off to be sure the rest of the place was clear. After removing all of the dope boy's guns, Rob and TJ began confiscating the money and dope in view, tossing it into a backpack they had brought along. Solo came escorting a fourth dope boy from the bedroom into the front room with his Glock .40 pressed to the back of the dope boy's skull and shoved him down onto the floor with the others. And Bone returned after clearing the place.

"Where the stash at? Huh?!" Rob demanded and kicked one of the dope boys in his ribcage. Everyone kept quiet.

Blam! Blam!

Bone didn't even think twice before shooting one of the dope boys once in each leg. "Talk, nigga!"

"A'ight, a'ight!" the bullet wounded dope boy cried out pleadingly as Bone aimed the gun at him again. He wanted to avoid being shot again.

"It's in the kitchen stashed in the bottom of the stove."

"Y'all watch these mu'fuckas while I go and snatch up the stash real quick," Bone said before turning for the kitchen.

A moment later, Bone returned from seizing the stash then he and the others began heading out. As they headed for the door, Max stood holding the marks at gunpoint to be sure none of them tried anything as they cleared out. Suddenly another unexpected dope boy popped out from the adjacent bathroom aiming a handgun and let off.

Blocka! Blocka! Blocka! Blocka!

"Argh, shit!" Max cried in pain from taking a bullet in his left leg.

With no hesitation, TJ turned his Glock .17 with an extended clip on the armed dope-boy and sent shots through him, causing the dope-boy to crash back into the wall and slide down, leaving a trail of blood smeared going down the wallpaper. TJ had murked the dope boy, saving Max from meeting an early death. Furiously, Max opened fire on the helpless marks, leaving some wounded and others dead.

"Let's get the fuck outta here," Solo called out to the gang.

Rob unsuspectingly turned his aim on Solo and stated, "Too bad you won't be makin' it outta here alive." He glared into Solo's eyes and squeezed the trigger.

Boc!

The fatal shot to Solo's dome splattered his noodles, and his dead body dropped to the floor with a thud. The whole time, Rob's ploy was to double-cross Solo, unbeknownst to any of the others. Leaving Solo dead as Rob n'em hurriedly exited the trap house, Bone assisted Max out to the Lexus parked at the curb. TJ hopped into the driver's side, and Rob took up shotgun while Bone and Max filled the backseat. Once they were all inside the SUV, then TJ skirted off.

"Max, you a'ight back there?" Rob asked in concern.

"It's nothin' but a flesh wound," Max replied, nursing his wounded leg.

"He's a soldier, so he'll be a'ight," Bone chimed in.

"Bone, it was on you to make sure the rest of the fuckin' house was clear. We could have gotten smoked!" TJ said heatedly as he shifted the SUV through traffic.

"But neither of us got smoked, so miss me with that shit, TJ!" Bone remarked.

"Look, Max will live. So, TJ and Bone, chill the fuck out," Rob intervened. "We got what we came for. Bone, put the stash you collected in the bag with the rest of the take." He passed the backpack back to Bone, who only put a portion of what he collected in the bag unbeknownst to the others. Rob added, "We'll sell all of the dope and then divide all of the money."

If only Rob and the others knew that Bone had already clipped some of the money, then they would know that there is no honor amongst thieves.

•••

"Are you fuckin' serious right now?" Rich said into his iPhone while sitting on the edge of the bed.

"That's exactly what one of our boys who was at the club last night told me went down," Tay-Mac replied, referring to the escapade Don was involved in outside of the 618 Nightclub. "One of the pack-boys happened to be on the club scene when the shit went down and had reported it to me. And now I'm makin' you aware just in case some heat came out of it from either cops or opps."

Rich shook his fuckin' head. "Look, I'll have a talk with Don about this shit. We can't have him bringin' so much attention to us with all the jewels, cars, and beefs if we're gonna run the game. He's just my big bro and all, but I won't just sit back at let him be our downfall after we did so much to rise to the top. Just keep your ear to the streets." He ended the call.

After a long day of trappin', Rich was at home when he received the call from Tay-Mac in the wee hours of the morning. Part of him was heated as hell at Don, but for the most part, he was relieved that it wasn't a call about Don being left dead instead. Rich knew it was best to have a talk with Don about his way of living before it was too late, one way or another. Better late than never, he contemplated.

He was in bed with ol' girl, Brittany, that he had recently met, and she lay beside him now awake. Over the past couple of months, they had grown quite acquainted with one another. Rob admire that she was a student at Marquette University, majoring in criminology in the hopes of becoming a lawyer someday. Brittany was attracted to the fact that he was a hood-nigga with dreams to make it out the hood. They were enjoying every moment of their acquaintance.

Brittany slid up behind him and wrapped her arms around his neck. "Is everything okay?"

"It's just my big brother. He's up to his usual shit," Rich stressed.

"And what're you gonna do about him?"

Rich sighed. "All I can do is let him know that he needs to tone it down some and hope that he'll understand."

"If he knows that you're only trying to lookout for the best of all of you, then he will."

"You're right," Rich concurred.

"Now, are you gonna talk about your brother all night or are you gonna fuck me?"

Rich smirked. "Enough about bro for the night."

"Then why don't you fuck me."

Brittany began kissing Rich over his shoulder as she slid her manicured hands down his bare chest and slipped a hand inside his boxer briefs, fondling his dick. Rich's dick grew large and stiff in Brittany's hand as she stroked it slowly. He laid her back in bed and mounted her, pulling her panties off and tossing them on the floor with his own underwear. Her pussy was wet, and Rich slipped two fingers inside and began massaging her clit. Enjoying the pleasure of her clit being caressed, Brittany softly moaned. Rich smoothly replaced his fingers with his piece, taking his time sliding every inch into her twat. While Rich stabbed his dick in and out of the pussy, Brittany raked her nails over his back out of pleasure.

"Damn Britt, this pussy the truth," Rich grunted in close to a whisper. He grabbed her legs and pushed them back over her head, and dug deep in her. "You like that shit, baby, huh?"

"Yaaas... You're so damn deep in this pussy," Brittany moaned. She bit down on her lower lip while watching as his large dick slid back and forth in her wetness.

Rich climbed out of bed and pulled Brittany to its edge while he stood in between her agape legs, fuckin' her pussy to his own beat. She laid back, sucking her own titties and enjoying the pleasure that he brought her. The feeling of her pussy walls gripping at his hardness brought Rich to climax. He pulled out and then squirted his semen on her stomach. Afterwards, Rich knelt between her legs and tongued her pussy. He used his fingers to spread her pussy lips, exposing the clit, and began massaging it with his tongue.

"Mmm, oooh... You're eating me so fuckin' good, Rich!" Brittany cried out in pleasure. She palmed the back of his head and pushed his mouth onto her pussy more.

"And you taste good, boo." Rich slurped and sucked on her wetness, causing her to arch her back off the bed. He ate her until she creamed in his mouth.

Following their fuck session, Rich lay in bed holding Britt. Though he was there with her, his mind was on Don's whereabouts. He just hoped that no heat would come back on them for the beef at the club. Possible beef like that is why he had turned down Don's offer to hit up the club to just focus on trappin'. Besides, he felt like fuck the club because he would rather count a million bucks.

•••

Reaching into the backseat, Rob grabbed the backpack which contained the dope he and his gang hit the lick for with a now-dead Solo the night prior. He and the others stepped out of the Lexus SUV and then headed towards the trap house to meet with the drug boss Heavy.

After knocking on the back door, a moment later, they were permitted inside by a nigga with a strap on his waist and its extended clip protruding. Rob and the others were led into the basement, where there was the stench of weed and liquor.

Rob stepped over to Heavy, who was seated on the couch, and his gang flanked him all on ten. He tossed the bag in Heavy's lap and said, "Inside, it's a block and a half. And it's yours for forty Gs."

"So, who'd you lay down for this work?" Heavy probed.

"All you need to know is now it's yours," Rob told him.

"It's like that?"

"Straight like that."

Heavy unzipped the bag and pulled out the individually packaged coke. "Yo Swindle, why don't you go and grab

Rob the paper he's askin'," he instructed, and Swindle rose from the couch and stepped away to grab the money.

The two had an arrangement. Whenever Rob hit licks, any work he came up on was sold to Heavy for the low. And Heavy saw it as a win-win. Not only was he getting low-priced supply, but his competitors were also being wiped out. And though they both had different hustles, they benefited from one another. Most jack-boys and dope-boys didn't do much business together, but Rob and Heavy respected each other's hustles.

Once Swindle returned, he handed Rob the stacks of cash wrapped with rubber bands. The two exchanged glares. They obviously had a disliking for one another. Although thus far, they didn't have any problems. If so, then neither wouldn't have hesitated to solve it with a bullet.

"It's all there," Swindle assured with a brisk tone.

"It better be," Rob replied assertively as he stuffed the stacks into his pockets without bothering to give it count. Just as fast as he came, he and his gang turned and made an exit.

Swindle looked to Heavy. "Dawg, I got reason to believe it was Rob and his team who laid down the gamble spot and took my chain. We gotta watch our backs for that nigga," he suggested.

"Swindle, how can you be sure of that?" Heavy asked.

"Just the look in his eyes. You sure Rob isn't plottin' to take you, Heavy?"

"Only thing I'm sure of is ain't no nigga takin' mine."

CHAPTER 10

The girls were in the hair salon. Shanta and Kat sat under hairdryers while Parker laid back with her head in the sink, getting her hair washed by Trina. Afterwards, Parker took a seat under a hairdryer also. Trina busied herself prepping her station to do some hair while the girls' hair dried.

Kat noticed Parker smiling at whatever she was looking at on her iPhone. "Bitch, what got you cheesing so hard and shit?" she wanted to know.

"More like who," Shanta corrected, peeping that Parker was checking out pics of a nigga on her Snapchat site.

Parker turned her phone out of sight. "You two bitches are so damn nosey!" she half-joked.

"And who is that nigga?" Kat probed.

"Whoever he is, his ass is fine," Shanta input.

"He's just a nigga I been getting to know on Snapchat for a few weeks. His name's Castle," Parker told her girls.

She had met Castle when he had stopped for a quick bite to eat at the McDonald's she managed, and ever since, they mostly communicated on social media. "So far, he and I haven't gone out on a date, but he has asked me out already."

Shanta shifted towards her. "You accepted, right?"

"No, I didn't."

"And why didn't you, Parker?"

"I don't want to rush into anything, that's why."

"Girl, you need to rush into his bed because you can use a man in your life," Kat commented.

Shanta cut her eyes at Kat. "Don't listen to this thot. Take your time, boo," she told Parker. "What type of nigga is he anyway?"

"Girl, the nigga is a baller! And I can tell he's a dope boy. He owns his own home, has three foreign cars, and stays iced out. Not to mention that judging by the pics, not only is he fine as hell, but he also has a big dick!" Parker beamed.

"So, are you going to share those pics, or what?" Kat asked.

"Uh, no, bitch. They're for my eyes only," Parker responded.

Kat smacked her lips. "Be that way then."

"Kat, your ass is a mess. You just want to see how big the nigga dick is." Shan laughed.

"Maybe if you get your own man, then you can see your man's dick all you want," Parker added.

"Whatevs!" Kat rolled her eyes.

Parker shifted towards both her girls. "Seriously though, I really like Castle. Not just because he has money. Mainly because he seems like a good nigga." She was into Castle, and apparently, he was into her. He seemed to like her type of nigga, and she wanted to be the type of bitch he needed. However, Parker didn't want to rush into anything with him, so she'd just take time getting to know Castle. She really didn't know what she was in for.

Once Parker's hair was dry, Trina escorted her back over to her station, where Parker took a seat in the salon chair. "What'll it be, girl?" she asked Parker, referring to her hairstyle of choice.

"Why don't we do something new?"

"A new look for your new man, huh? Okay, I got you. Just sit back and relax."

One thing about Trina, she never missed any of the gossip around the shop. Little did any of the girls who routinely came there know, she always had an open ear with a hidden agenda.

After doing her client's hair, it was time for Trina to get off work. She checked the time on her iPhone. As usual, Rob was late picking her up. Through the picture window of the shop, she saw Rob's Hellcat slide to the curb out front. Trina grabbed up her Prada bag, then exited the shop. She entered the whip and slammed the door shut with a thud, then thrust back in the passenger seat with her arms folded. Rob just puffed on the blunt as he pulled into traffic and zipped the Hellcat down the street.

"Don't slam my damn door like that again, Trina. What's your problem?" Rob asked, really not giving a fuck.

"You're late," Trina answered with attitude.

"Maybe next time you can just take a damn Lyft because I didn't have to come to pick your ass up."

Trina shifted towards him and said, "Look, thanks for picking me up. I just hate it when you have me waiting." She pouted.

"It pays to be patient, Trina. I learned that from havin' to patiently wait for the right moment to lay niggas down." Rob smirked.

"Good to know because I have a nigga for you to lay down. But it's going to take some time and patience while I gather more details on him," Trina told him.

"Take your time, and I'll be patient," Rob said. "Now, suck on a nigga's dick."

"M'kay, daddy."

Trina pulled Rob's dick out of his Blue Bands Only stonewashed denim jeans, then slipped it in her mouth and sucked it to hardness. He puffed the blunt while she gave him lip service as he tried to keep from crashing the whip. She flicked her tongue over the tip of his dick while jacking its base in her hand. Rob enjoyed the feel of her sexy mouth pleasing his dick. She sucked and slurped, giving him sloppy-toppy. He pulled to a stop at a red light, and the motorist idled beside him in traffic got a glimpse of Trina orally pleasing him.

"Shit, boo. Your mouthpiece so right," Rob groaned. He puffed the blunt while resting his back against the headrest as Trina faced him.

"Mmmm..." Trina moaned as she deep throated Rob's joint and fondled with his sac. She could tell he was on the verge of bustin' a nut, so she sucked his dick aggressively. Moments later Rob busted a nut in her mouth, and she licked the dick clean before replacing it inside his jeans.

Rob puffed the blunt once more and then passed it to Trina. "For that lip service, maybe I'll be on time from now on whenever I have to pick you up again," he said, wearing a smirk as he pulled off with traffic once the light flipped green.

•••

Rich slid through the hood in his newly purchased red Lexus coup. He spotted Don posted out on the block and then veered his whip to the curb and stepped out. Not liking how Don had been causing them unwanted attention lately with all his glazin', Rich felt it was best to tell Don he needed to tone it down.

Don stood amongst a few of his boys as Rich approached. "Haven't seen you in the hood lately, Rich."

"Knew I'd find you here. Don, we need to talk. Alone," Rich told him.

"Whatever it is you need to talk with me about, my boys can hear it too."

Rich eyed him a moment. "Been hearin' a lot about you in these streets glazin' and shit. And what's up with the shit that took place at the club, Don?"

"Look, I'm just doin' me in these streets. If a mu'fucka don't like it, then fuck 'em. As for the club incident, nigga got what his ass had comin'." Don snorted.

"You can do you without bringin' so much unneeded attention. All I'm sayin' is you need to keep a low profile because we don't need haters or cops all over us."

"Rich, fuck a hater and a cop. I won't let neither prevent me from glazin', whether you like it or not."

"I'm just tryna look out for you and me both. But apparently, you're too damn selfish to realize that. Just don't drag me down with you," Rich told him.

Don scoffed. "Either you with me or against me, Rich."

"I'm with you, Don. Although, I'm against your bullshit." Rich turned for his whip. Once he hopped inside, he smashed off. He didn't want there to be a wedge between him and his brother, but he wasn't willing to go along with Don's nonsense.

Don knew that his brother wasn't much of the flashy type of nigga as much as he himself was. But the way Don saw it is he was willing to accept what came with his street fame.

Don parked the Range in front of his loft complex. He offed the engine and then rested his head back against the headrest. What Rich had said to him about needing to tone it down slid through his mind. *Who the fuck is he to tell me how to live my damn life?* Don mused, seething. What bothered him most was that Rich made it seem like it was mainly his fault that cops and opps had it out for them. Don failed to realize that it was all his unnecessary attention that had all eyes on them. Or maybe he just liked the recognition of being a Trap God.

Don stepped out of the Range, closed its door, and then headed inside the complex. He entered the loft and found Shanta wearing only a sheer red negligée and Gucci stilettos.

There were plates of food and candles set out on the table, and the lights were dimmed. She wanted to surprise him with a special night of catering to his wants and needs since he did so much for her. "Hey baby, I'm glad you're home," Shanta said, wearing a smile. She waltzed up to him, wrapped her arms around the nape of his neck, and pulled his lips onto hers. She sensed that something was wrong. "What's wrong, Don, don't you like all of this?" she referred to her wears and the candle-lit dinner.

Don sighed. "Hell yeah, I like it, baby."

"Then what's wrong, because I did all of this for you."

"It's not you, Shan. A'ight." He was frustrated. "My bad. It's just I had a talk with my l'il bro today, and he was all over me about my lifestyle and shit."

"Why don't you have a seat." She grabbed his hand in hers and led him over to the table where she helped him into his seat, and then she sat on his lap. "Now, tell me all about your talk with Rich."

"He thinks my way of livin' is bringin' us heat. He even mentioned the shit that took place at the club the other night and tried makin' it seem like it was my fault. He says I need to tone down a bit. Can you believe that shit?" Don scoffed.

"Baby, whether you want to believe it or not, maybe Rich has a point about your flashy lifestyle."

"Not you too."

"I'm just saying that maybe you should listen to your brother on this."

"Then I'll listen to him when he listens to me about Mama," Don replied.

"Don, your mom has nothing to do with this. This is between you and Rich. If anything, you two need to come together on the strength of your mom," Shanta told him.

Don knew she was right, although he rather be stubborn. "Well, I'ont see that happenin' unless Rich sees things my way," he breathed.

"You're so damn stubborn."

"It be like that sometimes."

Shanta shook her head. "Anyway. How about you have some dinner."

"Bae, this dinner looks good and all, but I rather we skip right to dessert," Don said, wearing a smirk.

Shanta began kissing Don, slipping her tongue into his mouth. She dropped onto her knees in between his legs, pulled his dick from his Blue Bands Only jogger pants, jacked it to hardness, and then sucked on it. Her tongue slid up and down the shaft of his dick, and then she took its full length into her mouth.

"Damn, bae... Your l'il bad ass doin' that!" Don groaned. He was so turned on by Shan gazing up into his eyes as she chewed him hungrily. Her tongue swirled around the tip of his dick as she worked her soft lips on its head while jacking the saliva-coated shaft in her hand. Her mouth felt so damn good to Don, and he allowed his head to fall back as he enjoyed the feel of her sucking him. She worked her mouth so good on his dick that he couldn't help but nut in her mouth, which she swallowed.

Shanta then rose and pushed her panties to the side as she straddled Don in the chair and slid her pussy down on his dick. She placed her hands on either shoulder and bucked up and down on the dick, feeling it deep in her. Don sucked her titties while palming her ass, and she tossed back her head in pleasure as she rode him.

"Uhhhn...mmmm, yesss! I'm about to cum, Don!" Shanta uttered, feeling an orgasm wave within her.

Don stood while holding Shanta and set her atop the table. He knelt in between her agape legs then began eating the pussy like it was dessert. He spread her pussy lips with his fingers in order to suck and lick on her clit, causing Shanta to arch her back. She palmed the back of his head and pressed his mouth on her pussy.

"That's it, bae! Oooh... I'm cummmin!" Shanta purred as she creamed in Don's mouth.

Don rose onto his feet and kissed Shanta, allowing her to taste her own juices. He met her eyes and said, "Now, let's go and take a shower."

CHAPTER 11

Rich held open the door for Brittany, allowing her to enter the hookah lounge. As Brittany stepped by him, she slightly grazed Rich, and he enjoyed the tease of her touch and the aroma of her Chanel perfume. While he admired her ass, she peered back over her shoulder at him, all but expecting he would.

He thought she was looking so damn good in her form-fitting thigh-high white Louis Vuitton dress and yellow slingback heels, which matched her clutch purse, and rockin' her hair draping in inches. And she thought he cleaned up well in his Fendi V-neck sweater shirt and distressed blue jeans with Fendi sneakers. They made for a good-looking couple. Tonight was their first date.

They had stopped by the lounge after leaving the comedy club where their date night had begun. The atmosphere was everything, dimly lit, and the music in the background was soothing. Rich led Brittany to a secluded table, where he pulled out her chair and allowed her to take a seat before he sat across from her. He gestured over a waitress and ordered them each a glass of Hennessey on the rocks.

Rich and Britt had gotten to know each other better over the past month. They spent most of their time talking via texts and on FaceTime whenever they weren't together. And Rich took a great deal of a liking to Brittany. He thought she was smart and sexy. He could see himself with her. And he was sure to show her just how much he was feelin' her. Brittany had to admit that she was so into Rich. She admired that he was down to earth and fine as hell. And she wouldn't mind being with him. They weren't in an exclusive relationship, but the couple seemed right for each other, and they liked it that way.

Leaning back in his chair and taking in Brittany with his eyes, Rich said, "Hope you're havin' a good time with me so far."

"Actually, I am. The comedy show was lit. And this place is nice," Brittany replied. "And how about you, are you having a good time?"

"As good as it gets. Unless it gets better by the end of the night."

Brittany smiled. "Maybe."

"Good to know."

The waitress returned with their drinks, and Rich tipped her before she went on his way. He grabbed up his drink, and as he took a swig from the glass, he eyed Brittany over its rim. She noticed his eyes caressing her and found herself blushing.

"What?" Brittany asked shyly.

"I'm just tryna figure out why a girl like you has been single for so long," Rich said.

Britt sipped at her Henny. "And what kind of girl do you take me as?"

"A girl who knows what she wants."

"Which is exactly why I was single. Because I do know what I want in a man, and I wasn't willing to settle for less."

"So, do you think a man like me is worthy?"

"Rich, I think a lot of you. There's something about you that seems different from most men," Brittany told him.

"And you're nothin' like most girls, Brittany. I think it's attractive that you know your worth," Rich responded.

Brittany sat her glass atop the table. She quirked her arched brow and said, "And lemme guess, you were single because you love the streets too much."

Rich took a swig from his glass. "No. I was single 'cause I haven't met a girl who I can love more than the streets."

"What is it about the streets that you love so much?"

"For the most part, the streets raised me when my parents weren't able to."

"And what about your parents, where were they?"

"Look, you and I come from two different lives, so you wouldn't understand. You were raised by parents who loved you and all. While mine never seemed to care. So, it was the streets that raised me to be a rich savage," he expressed.

"But there's more to life than the streets raised you."

"Like what?"

"Like whatever you put your mind to, Rich. Listen, I just want you to know your worth. I'm not trying to change you," she expounded.

Rich reached across the table and grabbed her manicured hand in his. "Brittany, I'ont mind change for the better. So..." In that moment, Rich's words trailed off when he noticed Don entering the lounge with Shanta on his arm. Once noticing Rich there, Don made his way over to Rich's table.

"Didn't expect to see you here, Rich," Don said flatly.

Shanta nudged Don and told him: "Don't be that way." She looked to Rich. "Hey, Rich. Who's your friend here?"

"My name's Brittany," she introduced herself.

"Hi, girl. I'm Shanta. Nice to meet you." She checked out Brittany's appearance. "And those slingbacks are cute!"

Brittany held a foot out and replied, "Oh, these old things. They're Louie V."

"Mind if Don and I join you two?"

"Actually," Rich rose from his seat, "we were just leavin'. But maybe we can get together some other time." He helped a confused Brittany out of her seat.

Don scoffed and shook his damn head. "Go ahead, Rich, leave. Just make sure you at least go see your mama," he told him.

Rich eyed him and said, "Don, I'll see her whenever she's at her best. Until then, she shouldn't expect to see me. So, let it go." He pulled out some cash and left it on the table to cover his and their fees. "It's on me. You two enjoy your night."

Don watched as Rich made his way out of the lounge. He then turned to Shanta, who just shook her head and took a seat at the table. Don sat without a word, knowing Shanta didn't approve of how he came at Rich. A waitress showed up and took their orders.

As Rich sped the Lexus through traffic, his mind sped right along. He couldn't help but think about what Don said about his mama; should he go see her? Brittany could tell he had something on his mind. She figured it had to do with the guy Don back at the lounge and wondered about him. Rich and Brittany rode in silence with Moneybagg Yo's tune, "Hard for the Next", playing at a modest volume in the background. Both held thoughts of their own.

"Rich," Brittany opened, breaking the silence. "Mind telling me why you wanted to leave the lounge suddenly?"

"I rather not be around Don," Rich told her while keeping his eyes straight ahead on traffic.

"And who's Don to you?"

"Don's my big bro."

"Doesn't seem like you're brothers."

"Well, lately, I haven't been feelin' much like my brother's keeper," Rich admitted. He swerved around a vehicle.

Brittany shifted towards him in her seat. "You never seem to talk about your brother. And let alone your mother. How come?"

"Look, it's just that I rather not." He glanced over at her and said, "Maybe some other time I'll tell you all about it."

"Okay. Whenever you feel the time's right."

Rich steered with his left hand and planted his free hand on her exposed thigh. "Thanks for understandin'."

"You're welcome." She smiled.

Arriving at Brittany's place, Rich pulled the Lexus to the curb. Neither one of them wanted the night to end. They'd enjoyed one another's company and found that they cared for each other's companionship.

Rich walked Brittany to her front door. "My bad if I ruined the night. How about I make it up to you if you'll let me?"

"Sounds good. Maybe next time we can just stay in, watch movies, and order takeout."

"Sounds like a plan," Rich agreed. He grabbed her at the waist and pulled her in for a kiss. Their lips linked, and tongues met. His dick stiffened, and her pussy moistened. They wanted each other.

Brittany pulled back. "Rich... I got to get up early for work tomorrow. Just call me whenever you get home," she said, finding it hard to resist him. "Good night."

Once Brittany entered her place, Rich turned for his whip. He dispelled down the street, wondering if he could love Brittany more than he does the streets.

•••

Angie stepped out of the rehab center three months clean, and Don was there to pick her up. Once successfully completing the twelve-step sobriety program, she was discharged. After being an addict for most of her life, Angie didn't know what she was going to do with herself now that she was sober. Don wanted her to know that she didn't have to take on life alone, and Angie appreciated his love and support. However, she was ready to turnover a new leaf.

Don wrapped Angie into his embrace and kissed her forehead. "Ma, I'm so proud of you!"

"I couldn't have done it without you, Donte," Angie replied with discontent in her voice.

"Thought you'd be excited. What is it?"

"Don't get me wrong, I am excited. It's just that I wish your brother was here too."

Don sighed. He had texted Rich earlier with the hopes of Rich also showing up to support their mom, but apparently, Rich failed to show. Don knew that their mom really wanted Rich to see her now clean in the hopes that it would change things for the better between them. And Don could see that Angie was hurt that Rich hadn't shown up.

"Ma, I'm sorry Rich isn't here. But don't let it ruin this moment for you. I got you a surprise that I'm sure will cheer you," Don told her.

"A surprise? What is it?"

"Wouldn't be a surprise if I told you. C'mon."

Don ushered her into the Range before hopping in himself and pulling off. He wanted to surprise her with something that she wouldn't expect. Subsequent to leaving the rehab center, they pulled into the driveway of a redbrick house walled in by eight-foot hedges. The home was located in the suburbs of West Allis, far away from the hood they were used to. The inside of the home had four bedrooms and two baths, and it was fully furnished. Don had purchased the eighty-thousand-dollar home for Angie. He wanted to get his mom out of the hood, which was a dope boy's dream.

"Ma, this is your surprise," Don told her.

"Oh, my goodness!" Angie gasped at the sight of the charming home. "It's beautiful."

"Why don't we go and take a look inside."

96

Don exited the Range and then stepped around and opened the passenger door for his mom. He then handed her the keys to the home, and she walked up to the oakwood front door and slid the key into the door lock, and then entered the home. The inside of the home was fully furnished. Angie thought it looked like something out of a magazine. She sat on the white leather couch in the front room, overwhelmed with emotions.

"I love it, Don. Thank you," Angie said in close to a whisper.

"No need to thank me, ma. I told you, once you get clean, I'd take good care of you," Don replied. He took a seat beside her. "As much as you may not believe it, you deserve this and more. I just want you to really get your life together, and as long as you stay clean, I'm sure you'll be able to do whatever you would like. And I'm here for you."

"Baby, I don't know what I would do without you," Angie told him. She shifted towards him. "Maybe it's best that you get out of the game before it's too late for you and Rich."

"Ma, we ain't about to have this discussion again. I get that you want better for Rich and me, but the game has been good to us. Listen, don't worry so much about Rich and me. Besides, I already told you that I'd look after him."

"And who's going to look after you?" Angie asked, giving Don something to ponder.

At that moment, without knocking on the front door, Rich entered the home. Don was just as surprised as Angie to see him there.

"When I stopped at the center and you were gone, I figured that I would find you here," Rich said as he closed the door behind himself.

Don stood. "Good, you showed up. I wasn't sure you would," he admitted.

"Me neither. But after considerin' it, I understand how much today means to all of us. Especially mama."

"And here I was believing you didn't care about my sobriety. I'm glad you came," Angie expressed to Rich.

"Ma, you can believe that you gettin' clean is a proud moment. But it still doesn't make up for all the time missed."

"I understand that I can't make up for lost time. Although now I'm hoping that I can spend as much time as I can with both of you." Angie rose to her feet and stepped towards him. "Richard, while I had to be in the center, I thought a lot about how much my drug addiction affected my life over time. The main thing I found myself thinking about is how it affected my relationship with you and your brother. I can't apologize enough for not being there, but if it's worth anything, I'm here for you now."

Rich held mixed emotions concerning his mom. He met her sorrowful eyes and said, "Look, Ma, as long as you stay clean, then we can work on our relationship. I know that I haven't always been sympathetic towards you, but it never meant that I don't love you."

"Baby, you don't know how much hearing that means to me," Angie said. She hugged Rich, and he hugged her back. "I love you too, Richard. I always have."

Rich just hoped that he and his mom could mend their relationship moving forward. As much as he'd resented her over the years, Rich always wanted better for Angie. He hoped that she would stay clean. And he admired that Don helped her along the way. However, there were still some unresolved issues between him and his brother.

"Good to see you two gettin' along," Don said as he stepped up.

"I'm glad to have both of you as my sons. I know that I haven't been the best mother, however that will change.

Thanks to you both, I was able to find the strength to get myself clean. So, on the strength of me, I need you two to always be there for one another," Angie expressed. Tears rimmed her eyes.

Don and Rich looked at each other. As of lately, they hadn't been on the same track. But at that moment, they both knew their mom was right.

"Don't worry, Ma, me and Rich will have each other's backs," Don assured.

"Don and I will face anything together," Rich added.

"Good." Angie was happy to hear her sons were together.

Rich grabbed Angie's hand. As he led her towards the front door, he said, "Ma, since Don bought you a home, I figured I would get you somethin' also." When they stepped outside, there parked in the driveway was a sleek black Jaguar SUV.

Angie gasped. "It's nice!"

"Glad you like it."

"Boys, I can't thank you enough for doing all of this for me." Angie went to get a closer look at her new ride.

"Never thought I would see the day you forgive our O.G.," Don told Rich.

"She may not have been the best mom, but like you always tell me, she's the only one we get. So, I just want to give her a chance."

"And what about us?" Don wanted to know.

Rich eyed his big brother. "Don't get it misunderstood. This doesn't change things between us. I'm only here for moms."

Angie overheard her son's discussion, and she couldn't bear the thought of them having differences. She just hoped they would figure it out and soon because she wanted for Don and Rich to always be their brother's keeper.

Martell "Troublesome" Bolden

CHAPTER 12

As T-Mac sucked barbeque sauce off his fingers, he noticed Rich hardly touched his slab of ribs and just knew that Rich had something on his mind. Whenever they came to this particular barbeque joint, Rich normally enjoyed the food. But today seemed different.

The two sat in a booth eating their meals. They had stopped at the barbeque joint for a bite to eat after dropping off the product and picking up profits from a couple of the trap spots. Their gang had no problem moving the few birds they were now coppin' from the plug, and the paper started to pile up. The only thing Rich wanted was for the crew to keep a low profile, so they don't have to worry about the operations being interrupted in any way.

"What's on your mind, Rich?" T-Mac probed.

"It's nothin'," Rich replied monotonously.

"It's obviously somethin'. So, what's up?" he pressed.

Rich leaned back in his seat. "It's all the shit with Don. He doesn't seem to get that what he does could affect the entire gang. Even when I advise him not to, Don still goes out and cop shit that's too flashy. It's like since I'm his l'il bro, he feels he shouldn't have to listen to shit I tell his ass," he stressed.

"I ain't sayin' it's cool but, Don's just doin' what most niggas who ain't never had shit do whenever they start countin' some real money."

"And what's that, let the money make them?" Rich snorted.

"Not Don; he's readymade. What I mean is niggas blow a bag on shit they been trappin' to have. Look, Don's not hurtin' anyone, so let him do him."

"What about that nigga at the club? He was left more than hurt, T-Mac," Rich said only loud enough for T-Mac to hear. "It's shit like that which brings all of us unnecessary attention. And I'ont know about you, but I'ont wanna have to watch my back for haters and cops."

T-Mac leaned forward and rested his elbows atop the table on either side of his plate of food. "Apparently, it was necessary that nigga got what he had comin' because I rather him than Don. And you don't have to worry about watchin' your back; that's what you got me for. A'ight?"

"A'ight. Even still, I worry about how shit will play out."

"Rich, what you need to worry about most is the next re-up. Maybe you should go along with Don and meet the plug this time around for yourself," T-Mac suggested.

"Since Don's takin' care of business with him, then I'ont have to meet the plug. As long as the work comes correct, then whoever this Castle nigga is all good with me," Rich replied.

"Say less. Now let's enjoy this good ol' barbeque." T-Mac wasted no more time returning to chowing down on his rib tips.

•••

Back at the trap spot in the hood, Don and Rich were there along with the others. The gang was getting their monies together for the re-up. Rich and C-Note sat at the kitchen table, counting up the bread, while Don and T-Mac wrapped each stack with rubber bands. And Danger loaded the cash inside a tote bag. After getting their money up off the first few flips, this time around, they were looking to cop five bricks from Castle.

There wasn't much being said between Don and Rich, and everyone could sense the tension. The brothers still hadn't been able to find common ground. Mainly due to both of them being stubborn. Realistically, they didn't like being at odds, but neither was willing to budge.

"What's up with you two niggas?" Danger said, referring to Don and Rich. "Y'all need to squash the beef."

Don leaned back in his chair. "It's Rich," he said.

"No, Don. It's you," Rich remarked.

"Well, whatever it is, y'all need to figure that shit out," C-Note piped in.

"And fast," T-Mac added.

Don looked to Rich. "Let's talk about this alone."

"Let's." Rich held Don's eyes without wavering.

Once Don stood from his seat, Rich followed suit. They both grabbed up their poles from the table and placed the weapons on their person before heading for the front door. With Don leading the way, he and Rich stepped outside onto the front porch. It was night outside, and the block was scarce while they stood visible beneath the dim porch light.

"You don't like how I'm doin' shit, then that's your problem, l'il bro," Don raved.

"Maybe if you stop doin' shit you do, then I wouldn't have a problem, big bro," Rich retorted.

"Look, I'ont see the problem with what I do, Rich. All that should matter is we're makin' more money now."

"That's just it; more money brings more problems. So, you see, now it's best to keep a low profile."

Don waved him off. "It is what it is."

"Don, will you just listen to me on this."

"I could say the same when it comes to mama."

"I guess that's your problem with me."

"Damn right it is, Rich. While you're concerned about what I'm doin', you haven't been concerned about mama much at all since she's been out of the rehab center. Maybe you should worry more about how she's doin' instead of me," Don told him.

Rich looked away down the block, which was mostly shrouded by darkness. "Let's not make this about mama, Don. If you wanna take care of her, then do you. But don't expect me to do the same when she didn't even care about us enough to raise us on her own," he expressed.

"Rich, maybe you need to let her know how you feel."

"Why? It isn't gonna change how I feel."

Don took a seat on the porch banister with his back towards the street while facing Rich. "Have you ever thought that maybe mama needed to know for herself? Believe me. She cares more than you know." He could see it on Rich's face that he was thinking on it.

"Don, I'ont wanna talk about mama right now. You need to just chill with glazin' and shit. We don't need anyone on our backs."

"I hear you, Rich. But-"

"Get down!"

Prraat- prraat- prraat- prraat!

Just as automatic gunfire erupted, Rich pulled Don down onto the porch. Rounds peppered the front of the house, some flying through windows. Glass particles sprinkled once a round shattered the porch light, which blanketed Rich and Don in darkness and made difficult targets out of them for the shooters. Without hesitation, Don pulled his .40 Glock as he rose to his feet and began firing back at the black SUV with a shooter standing out of its sunroof firing a Mac-11 at them. Rich hurried to his feet with his .26 Glock and leaped over the porch banister, firing at the SUV as it sped away down the street before sharply bending the corner. Neither Don nor Rich had gotten a good look at who the shooter was.

Rich stepped back onto the porch. "Who the fuck was that?" he wanted to know.

"Don't know. But whoever it was better pray I don't find out," Don swore.

The front door was snatched open, and C-Note and Danger were on either side of a blood-covered T-Mac, helping him outside in a hurry.

"T-Mac was shot!" C-Note cried out.

"We need to get him to a hospital now!" Danger implored.

"I-I'm not d-dyin' like this," T-Mac managed to vow through heavy breaths.

"And you won't die, T-Mac," Rich assured.

"Just stay with us, cuz, a'ight," Don encouraged him.

Once the automatic gunfire erupted outside, C-Note and Danger hit the floor while T-Mac went heading for the front door to check on his cousins. And when some rounds ripped into the house, then T-Mac was shot in the abdomen and left arm. When the shots subsided, C-Note and Danger rushed for the front door finding T-Mac crumpled on the front room floor in a pool of blood.

The gang rushed T-Mac over to Danger's Donk Chevy parked across the street at the curb. Rich pulled open its back door, then C-Note and Danger helped T-Mac inside the backseat. Danger jumped into the driver's side while Rich and Don sat in the back with their cousin, T-Mac's head lay in Rich's lap, and Don applied pressure to his bullet wound with T-Mac's Air Max sneakers across his lap. C-Note rode shotgun. He and Danger held their guns in hand just in case the shooters decided to spin on them once again. The gang sped down the street, heading for the nearest hospital in a rush.

"Faster, Danger!" Rich ordered. He didn't want T-Mac to die before they could get him some help to save his life.

"Goin' as fast as I can," Danger replied and then blared the horn at the vehicle ahead in traffic out of frustration before he swerved around it and zoomed through a yellow light.

"Did either of you see who the shooters were?" C-Note asked both brothers.

"If so, then we'll get at them niggas tonight," Danger told them as he shifted the Chevy through traffic.

Don quipped, "It was kinda hard to see who the mutha-fuckas were while we were dodgin' bullets and shit, a'ight."

"Maybe it was some of Tank's boys out for retaliation," Danger thought aloud.

"Or maybe it was some of Trip's boys," C-Note mentioned.

"Whoever it was, we need to find out and off 'em," Danger said.

"ASAP," C-Note added.

With all of their beefs in the streets, the gang couldn't exactly pinpoint who sent the shooters through to air out their trap house.

Don glanced over at Rich. "How's T-Mac holdin' up?" he asked, fearing the answer.

"He's barley breathin'," Rich said frantically.

"We're almost at the hospital, so don't trip."

Rich looked into T-Mac's eyes, who fought for each breath. "Just breathe, T-Mac!"

•••

"Now, what in the hell are we gonna do, huh?"

Heavy was worried about Don n'em finding out he was behind the futile hit, now knowing that they would be looking for answers. All Heavy wanted to do was get rid of Don to avoid a drug war so he could take over the drug trade in the hood. And had Swindle not missed Don, then Heavy would have shit his way.

Sitting at the wet bar in the basement of his trap house and gulping down shots, Heavy didn't know what to do. "Swindle, I left it up to you to handle Don," he sniped.

"And I will," Swindle assured. He sat beside Heavy on the bar stool. "I'm sure Don don't exactly know who tried to hit him, so we're good. And I'll make sure he never knows it was us."

"You think it's gonna be that easy to kill his ass now that he knows a target is on him."

"That's why we wait until he lets his guard down. And I know exactly how to get him to do that."

Heavy looked at Swindle then curiously asked, "How exactly?"

"Overlay for the underlay." Swindle smirked.

"You're forgettin' about Rich."

Swindle rubbed his chin. "Rich is the last one I'm worried about."

"Don't underestimate Rich, Swindle. He's gonna ride or die for his brother."

"Then he and Don can die together."

Swindle began to explain to Heavy how his ploy could work.

•••

After getting T-Mac to the hospital just in the nick of time, he had been rushed off to have surgery in order to remove a bullet lodged in his abdomen. Fortunately, it hadn't damaged any main organs, or he may not have lived long enough to have his life spared. While Don and Rich were in the emergency room waiting area, both painted with their cousin's blood, C-Note and Danger had rushed back to the trap to collect the re-up money left behind. After all of the blood shed, it felt like they were dealing with blood money.

"Listen, somethin' came up, so I'll have to get up with you another time to do business. Just give me a couple of days, and I'll get with you." Don ended the call with Castle after informing him their meet was off for the night. He was seated while observing Rich, who paced the waiting room floor with his mind racing. Once Rich started for the exit's automatic sliding doors, Don asked, "Where you goin'?"

Rich stopped in his tracks. "Outside away from you, Don," he remarked.

"And what's that s'pose to mean, Rich?"

"Means it's best that I not be around you right now before I say somethin' I can't take back."

"Go ahead..." Don stood to his feet and stepped into Rich's personal space. "Say it. Say it's my fault that T-Mac was shot. Say how you feel."

Rich shook his damn head and scoffed. "I ain't the type of nigga to say, 'I told you so, Don." He turned and headed out the exit with Don watching his back.

Don was sure Rich wouldn't let this go. And part of Don felt guilty about T-Mac being shot. He just had to find out who sent the hit and then kill his ass. Unbeknownst to Don or the others, they didn't have to go far to find the nigga.

CHAPTER 13

Angie locked the front door behind herself after she stepped out of her home. She then walked over to the driveway and chirped the car alarm on her Jaguar before she stepped inside. She was thankful that Don and Rich had looked out for her after she left the rehab center. And to show her thanks, she cooked them dinner every Sunday just to be around them in hopes of growing closer to both her sons. She understood it wouldn't make up for lost time, although her idea was to spend as much time as she could with Don and Rich.

Pulling out of the driveway, Angie set off heading to pick up some groceries. The sun shone down on the city as she cruised through traffic. Thus far, everything was going well for her. She'd been sober for nearly six months and now had a job working in a senior citizen's home as a receptionist. Her life was much better than before.

Arriving at her destination, Angie parked the Jag' in the parking lot of the Fast & Friendly convenience store, where almost everyone from around came for the deals on the meat, along with other purchases. This particular store was located in the hood she had raised her sons, which she hardly been to as of lately so to avoid any temptations. Plus, she knew her sons didn't like her being in the hood for certain reasons. But she needed to pick up some items and then would be on her way.

Angie stepped out of the car and then headed inside the store. She made her way to the meat department, where she placed an order. After purchasing a meat deal package along with a few other items, she exited. As Angie made her way to her car, she noticed the Chrysler with tinted windows that wasn't there before now parked beside her Jag'.

The passenger window dashed down, and there was Swindle. Just as Angie had been stepping out of her car, Swindle was pulling into the lot. So, he decided to wait outside for her.

"Been a while since I last saw you, Angie," Swindle said.

"I just been trying to get myself together, that's all," Angie replied.

"Well, I see you lookin' good and all. Even ridin' good." He couldn't help but notice that Angie looked better than usual. Her clothes weren't filthy, and she wasn't tweaking, so he figured she must have been sober.

"Yes, life is good for me right now."

"Look, we both know what's good for you, Angie." Swindle pulled out a sack of crack cocaine and held it up for her to see with the hopes that it would lure her in. *Once an addict, always an addict*, he thought vindictively.

It took everything in Angie to resist. "No. I can't. I'm clean now, Swindle. And I want to keep it that way. We both know if either Don or Rich knew about you offering me drugs, then they wouldn't like it. So just leave me be, will you," she told him.

Swindle scoffed. "Angie, whenever you're ready to get high, then you know where to find me. As for Don and Rich, they know I ain't hard to find."

With no further words, Angie entered her Jag' and then pulled out the parking lot. She knew it would be hard to fight her temptations to get high, especially with someone like Swindle pressuring her. But she'd do her best to remain clean because she didn't want to let down her sons. More importantly, she didn't want to let herself down.

Angie headed back home. It was near noon as Angie was cleaning her home. She was vacuuming the front room floor. Hearing the front door open and close, she looked back over her shoulder and found Rich. Angie offed the vacuum and then stepped over to Rich and pecked him on the cheek.

"Hey, baby. What brings you by?" Angie asked.

"Thought I'd drop by to see how you're doin'," Rich answered.

"I'm fine. Why don't we have a seat." Angie sat on the couch, and so did Rich. She knew his real reason for checking in on her. "You don't have to worry, Rich. I'm not here doing any drugs," she told him. Not wanting to worry her son, she decided not to mention her run-in with Swindle earlier.

Rich hunched forward, resting his arms on his knees. "Ma, I just wanna make sure you're really doin' good. If I didn't care, then I wouldn't even be here."

"I get it because your brother does the same thing. And I do appreciate that you two care about my well-being."

"Look, I know I haven't always been here for you like Don has, but I'm here now. It was never about him loving you more than me."

Angie shifted towards him. "Rich, you weren't wrong for being resentful towards me for choosing drugs over you and Don. Even though your brother may have been there, I never loved him more than I love you. No matter what, I love you two equally," she expounded.

"Good to know." It made Rich feel much better knowing his mom loved him even though he had once resented her.

"How are things with you and Don, by the way?" Angie was aware that her sons were still at odds, and she wanted them to find common grounds. Although, she wasn't going to get in the middle of them nor take sides.

Rich looked down at his hands and said, "Could be better. It's just Don seems to undermine me because I'm his l'il bro, even if I'm tellin' him what's right."

"Believe it or not, Don knows he needs you more than anyone to watch his back. You two are each other's keepers."

"I guess you're right." He met her eyes. "But part of me feels like he's the reason T-Mac was shot."

"Fortunately, T-Mac will be alright. But did you ever stop to think how it must make your brother feel that he may be the reason? I'm sure that's not easy on him at all. Try not to be so hard on him, Rich."

"For you, I'll try," Rich assured. "Look, Ma, I won't stay long. I'ont wanna leave my girl waitin'."

"Must be really into her if you care to be on time. Is she a good girl?" Angie probed.

"Her name's Brittany, and yeah, I think she's good for me." A smile spread across Rich's lips. "Brittany's smart and honest and bad! And you're right, Ma, I am really into her," he expressed.

Angie rubbed his thigh and said, "I'm happy you found a good girl in Brittany. I'm sure she feels the same about you."

"I'd like for you to meet her. I'm sure you'll like her, too."

"I'd like that. Just bring her over for Sunday dinner."

"Fa sho," Rich assured. He stood from the couch. "Ma, I'll see you for Sunday dinner, and I'll be sure to bring Brittany along."

"Alright. I look forward to it." She rose and then escorted Rich to the front door. "Stay safe out in those streets."

"I will." Rich pecked her on the cheek before he made an exit leaving Angie to her thoughts.

•••

There was a knock at the front door, and Brittany knew it was none other than Rich. As she headed to answer the door, she checked the surroundings of her plushy furnished apartment to be sure everything was as it should be. Brittany had the mood set with the lights down low. For the remainder of the evening, their plans were to watch Netflix and chill.

Once Brittany pulled open the door, she found Rich there wearing a smile with two boxes of Domino's pizza in hand. He admired how Brittany dressed comfy and somehow looked good in her fitted T-shirt and leggings, which showed off her juicy titties and phat ass. Her hair was in two French braids to the back, and she only wore lip gloss. Rich thought she was naturally beautiful. Keeping up with the comfortable vibe, he rocked a Blue Bands Only tracksuit and Air Jordan sneakers. His jewels only consisted of modest diamond earrings. Brittany thought he was as fine as it gets. It was apparent that they were very attracted to one another.

The two embraced and kissed before Brittany stepped aside, and Rich entered. He kicked off his Air Jordan's at the door, and then Brittany led him over to the black leather loveseat in the front room, and he set the boxes of pizza on the coffee table. She already had a bottle of Hennessey with two glasses and several blunts rolled up, all set out on the coffee table as well.

"Make yourself at home while I go and grab us some napkins," Brittany said. She headed for the kitchen with Rich admiring her ass.

She knows her ass phat, Rich thought to himself. He copped a squat on the loveseat and grabbed up a blunt, then set flames to it. He could tell the weed was some exotic as he puffed the blunt. Grabbing the TV remote, he played 'The Photograph' on Netflix. A moment later, Brittany returned and then took a seat beside Rich so they could chill. After the two shared the blunt while watching the movie, they dug into the pizza with the munchies. So far, they were enjoying each other's company.

"You got some sauce in the corner of your mouth," Brittany pointed out.

Rich wiped at the corners of his mouth with a napkin then said, "Did I get it?"

"No. I got you, though, boo." She used a thumb to wipe away the sauce and then sucked her thumb clean.

"Good lookin'." Rich shifted towards her. "You seem like the type of bitch who likes to cater to your nigga."

"Yeah, if he's worth it. But I want my nigga to take care of me in turn. It's give and take in a relationship."

"So, you have relationship goals."

"I do. How about you?" she wanted to know.

"More than anything, I just want a bitch that will appreciate a real nigga," he told her.

Brittany scooted near him and grabbed his hand, then wrapped it around her. "I know how to show my appreciation in so many ways." She got comfortable in his arms and felt like it was the right place for her to be.

"Britt, usually I'ont do this, but I want you to meet my mom."

"I'd love to."

"Good. I'm sure you'll like her."

Rich pulled her closer, and she molded into his arms. He loved having her all over him. Her Dior perfume was sensual in his nostrils, causing him to grow aroused. He grabbed her chin and guided her lips onto his. As their tongues danced around, Rich caressed Brittany's thigh, and her nipples grew hard against the fabric of her shirt. Brittany slipped a hand inside his tracksuit pants and fondled Rich's dick, causing it to stiffen. She then straddled his lap, and while they kissed, he gripped her ass in both hands. As he planted a trail of

114

kisses down her neck, she tossed her head back. Rich pulled her shirt off over her head, exposing her pretty titties, then he licked and sucked on her hard nipples causing her to set free soft moans. He stood from the loveseat while holding Brittany up by her ass and then lowered her back down onto the floor over the plush carpet. The two helped each other out of their bottoms. Brittany held her legs agape while Rich ate her pussy.

"Unh... Yes, eat it, baby!" Brittany groaned in pleasure as Rich flicked his tongue rapidly over her clit. She loved how he darted his tongue deep inside her pussy. "Mmm... I'm cummmmin!" As orgasm racked her body, her back slightly arched off the floor, and her toes curled.

Rich climb in between her legs and then slipped his dick inside her wetness. "Damn boo, this pussy so tight and wet," he said as he dug deep in her. She planted her manicured hands on either of his shoulders while she took the dick. Lowering his mouth onto hers, Rich kissed Brittany hungrily as he pounded at her pussy. She raked her nails over his back out of pleasure.

"Oooh, yaaas... That's my spot, Rich!" Brittany dug her nails into the flesh of his back as the tip of Rich's dick hit her G spot with each stroke. After some time, she wiggled from underneath him and positioned herself on all fours, and then Rich began fuckin' her doggy style.

"Whose pussy is this, huh? This my pussy, ain't it?" Rich wanted to know. While digging her out from behind, he held her ass steady.

"Yes! It's your pussy!" she cried. Looking back over her shoulder, she arched her back as Rich beat the pussy up. She was turned on seeing him bite down on his lower lip. "Mmm shit... Baby, I'm cumin again!" Brittany's twat oozed all over his dick, and her juices slid down his inner thigh.

Rich laid back on the floor, and Brittany mounted him sliding her wetness down onto his hardness. She planted her hands on his chest, and he gripped her ass as she bucked on the dick. Her head fell back, and she moaned in pleasure while bouncing on his pole. He slammed her up and down onto his dick, and she enjoyed the feeling of him digging in her love tunnel.

"Shit Britt, you got a nigga ready to bust. Ride this dick just like that," Rich grunted as Brittany put the pussy on him. She climbed off his dick and then wrapped her soft lips around its tip and sucked it into her warm mouth. He looked down into her eyes while she licked his balls and stroked the base of his dick in her hand. She slipped every inch of him in her mouth, and Rich bust a nut down her throat. "Damn boo, I see you a throat, baby." Rich grinned.

Brittany lay beside Rich on the carpet with a leg positioned over him. "I'll be whatever you want me to be," she smiled.

"In that case then, what I want you to be is my bitch."

"Instead, how about I be your bad bitch?"

Rich slid his hand down her back and rested it on her ass. "That's even better."

"I'm sure," Brittany said. She grabbed a blunt off the coffee table and then set flames to it, and after taking a puff, she stuck the blunt to Rich's lips, and he inhaled the thick weed smoke.

While the two lay on the floor in the nude and smoking the blunt, Rich couldn't help but think about how much he needed a bitch like Brittany in his life. He just didn't know if his lifestyle was for her.

CHAPTER 14

After three weeks of being on bed rest, T-Mac had been discharged from the hospital earlier in the day, and now he rolled with Rich. For the most part, T-Mac was healed, but he still remembered the hot sensation of the bullet he had taken. With the surgery to remove bullet fragments from his abdomen, T-Mac was left wearing a shit-bag. The way he saw it, that was far better than a body bag.

Rich pushed the Lexus through traffic while T-Mac rode shotgun and they were both strapped. They were on their way to meet with the others at the strip club. Instead of laying low, if a nigga gets popped and survives, it becomes a celebration.

"What, nigga?" T-Mac pressed after noticing Rich glance over at him for about the fourth time without saying a word.

"You a'ight, cuz?" Rich asked. He noticed T-Mac's head on the swivel.

"Yeah. I'm just bein' on point is all," T-Mac told him. After catching that fire, he was vigilant of his surroundings.

Rich patted his cousin's shoulder and stated, "Look, I got you. Even if I gotta be the one to take a bullet for you this time."

"Well, just know that bullets burn," he cracked.

"I guess you'd know," Rich chuckled. "Just glad your ass is still alive, cuz."

"Yeah, me too. But if you don't keep your eyes on traffic, that may not last long," he half-joked.

Rich dipped around an SUV while going nearly 40mph. "Don't worry. I won't crash."

"I'm more worried about Twelve pullin' us over. Look at how cops are killin' us for driving while Black. It's like they don't care that Black Lives Matter. Shit crazy." T-Mac shook his damn head.

"You right, that's why I'ont fuck with Twelve," Rich agreed. "Besides that, you should be worried about whoever tried to kill us that night. We still don't know who the hell it is."

"And on my life, whenever we find out who it is, then I'ma kill 'em," T-Mac swore.

"Until then, let's stay low and focus on gettin' paid." He turned, going eastbound on Silver Spring Avenue.

"Say no more. What about Don? He hadn't been to see me in over a week."

Rich glanced over at him and said, "I'm sure that's 'cause Don feels he's the reason niggas got it out for us and shit. He almost got you smoked. Told his ass he needs to tone it down."

"Rich, it's not Don's fault that I got popped. You know shit happens in this game, and I'm willin' to accept what comes with it."

"Well, he's the one who insisted we throw the celebration at the club. So, I'm sure he'll be happy to see you."

"Are you and Don good now, or what? I know y'all bumped heads over me takin' a bullet and shit."

"No, we bumped heads because had it not been for his ass doin' the most, then you woulda never taken a bullet."

"You can't look at shit like that, Rich. It's just part of the game, and I respect it. So, don't put the blame on Don because I don't," T-Mac told him.

"Maybe you're right. My girl, Brittany, also thinks I should make amends with Don."

"Sounds like Brittany's tryna tell you somethin'. Apparently, you're into shorty, seein' that you been spendin' a lot of time with her."

"Brittany's a good bitch. I just want things to go right with her because she's the kind of girl a nigga takes home to meet moms," Rich said.

"Then just make sure you treat her right," Tay-Mac advised. "By the way, has she met your mom yet?"

"Not yet. I ain't absolutely sure if I even want her to."

"Thought you were good with Auntie Angie now that she's clean."

"Somewhat. It's just, unlike Don, I still remember the past." Rich halted the whip at the stoplight. Positioned on the corner directly across the street was the strip club.

"Look, Rich," T-Mac started slowly. "Your O.G. isn't perfect, but she deserves for you to give her a real chance."

"Right. And I'm workin' on it," Rich said. "Now, let's go and enjoy ourselves."

Pulling into the parking lot of Red Velvet strip club, Rich parked the Lex'. He and T-Mac tucked their poles before the two stepped out of the car and then made their way into the club. Upon entering, the club scene was lit, there was a huge banner hanging which read: WELCOME HOME T-MAC! T-Mac was surprised to see almost everyone from their hood and crew were in attendance, including Heavy and Swindle.

T-Mac was greeted with tons of well wishes. Two bad-ass strippers approached T-Mac and took up either arm, then led him to the VIP section as Rich followed. They found Don, along with C-Note and Danger, all seated on the huge red velvet wraparound couch. They were all excited to see T-Mac. Mainly Don, because he hated the feeling of being the reason T-Mac nearly lost his life, even though he wasn't necessarily at fault. If anything, it was just part of the game.

"What's good, l'il cuz?!" Don hurried to his feet and greeted T-Mac with a thug-hug. "How you?"

"Aside from havin' to wear a damn shit-bag, I'm still breathin'." T-Mac grinned.

"And trust, when we find the nigga who popped you then, he gon' get popped like you got popped, but he ain't gon' be fuckin' breathin'," Don assured.

"Fa sho." T-Mac patted the pole on his waist. He wasn't going anywhere without it.

C-Note stepped up and gave T-Mac some dap. "Glad that you're still with us, homie. How shit was lookin', we thought it was curtains for you."

"Fa real, fa real," Danger added. He remained seated with a stripper in his lap. "And I still ain't forgivin' your ass for bleedin' all over my damn whip and shit."

"Dawg, stop jackin' like you wasn't the main one scared for my life. I heard your ass talkin' about 'stay up T-Mac, don't die T-Mac!'" T-Mac half-joked and they all shared a laugh.

"All jokes aside, let's not forget that shit was serious. And we all need to watch our backs until we find out who came for us," Rich told them.

Don grabbed a chilled bottle of Dom P. from the ice bucket on the table and handed it to T-Mac. "Let's not forget we're here to celebrate. Pour up!"

The gang sat on the couch, enjoying themselves as strippers entertained them. The owner of the club, who was a Trap God named Diamond, sent them some bottles on the house. There was a stripper giving them a table dance. She was standing bent over, gripping her ankles and clapping her phat ass while looking back at the boys through her gapped legs. While the gang was having a grand time, Don noticed Heavy attempting to enter their section, but he was stopped by a few of the gang members. Don whistled and got the members' attention, then gestured for them to let Heavy along with Swindle by. The whole gang had a thought that it was Heavy who sent the shooters that night, but they had no substantial evidence to prove it. However, if they found out it was Heavy, then he was as good as dead.

"I see y'all doin' it big in this mu'fucka tonight for T-Mac," Heavy commented, playing shit cool. "We look out for ours," Don responded.

Heavy looked to T-Mac and said, "Well wishes."

"Keep it for the nigga who popped me, 'cause he gon' wish he smoked me," Tay-Mac replied.

Swindle smirked. "Apparently, a bullet wasn't shit to you."

"Ain't gon' let a bullet change me." T-Mac turned the bottle up to his lips.

Swindle noticed T-Mac clutching the gun on his waist and said, "We ain't the ones you'll need the pole for."

"And what does that s'pose to mean?" Rich questioned aggressively.

"Means your boy can put the pole away 'cause we ain't the ones who you're lookin' for."

"Says who?" Don piped in.

"Says the streets. Word in the streets is it was Coop who aired out your spot. It's said he was out for revenge since Don allegedly had gotten Trip smoked," Swindle told them deceptively.

"And why should we believe that shit? Especially knowin' that you and Heavy had them niggas on the payroll behind our backs," Rich pressed.

"Because it's over money. After Trip was murked, Coop just assumed he didn't have to pay up for the work they loss to y'all. So, I figure he can pay back with his life."

"So, you want us to do you and Heavy's dirty work?"

"Nah, I'ont mind gettin' my hands dirty. A nigga can't mind it when he's handlin' dirty money, you feel me? I just thought you'd wanna handle Coop for yourself."

Rich gestured for T-Mac to remove his hand from the butt of his gun, and he obliged. Then Rich stated, "If I find out you're lyin', then I won't hesitate to handle you myself. A'ight?"

"Yeah, a'ight." Swindle was finna turn on his way, but then as an afterthought, he said, "Haven't seen Angie in a while in the hood. How's she?"

"Forewarnin', Swindle, stay away from my moms," Rich told him.

"Or you'll have to handle me and Rich," Don warned.

"Anyway," Heavy chimed in. "I just wanted to stop by and show my respect."

T-Mac eyed him sharply and stated, "Good. 'Cause I'll die for my respect."

"No doubt," Heavy said. "Y'all have a good one." He turned on his way, and Swindle shot the gang a smirk before following.

"Now what, cuz?" T-Mac asked as he observed Heavy and Swindle walk away.

"You know what." Rich shifted in his seat towards Don and said, "Somethin' tells me them niggas know more than they're lettin' on."

"How 'bout we down those niggas right now," Danger piped in and stood to his feet, ready to put in gun work.

"Be easy, Danger," Don told him, and then Danger sat back down. "We don't know if they know anything more."

C-Note stuffed some singles inside one of the stripper's G-string. "I'ont trust the nigga Swindle. He could be tryna set us up," he suggested.

"Or he could be tryna set Coop up," Danger added and then puffed the blunt.

"I'ont trust Swindle ass neither. But if what Swindle's tellin' us is the truth, then we can't just let Coop get away with comin' for us," Rich input.

Don sipped from his bottle of Dom P. "And Swindle could just be tryna mislead us. It's not like he and Heavy don't have a motive to come for us for the same reason. Maybe they're the ones who sent Coop because we stopped their side hustle," Don expounded.

Rich leaned back in his seat and eyed Don. "Don, do you always gotta go against whatever I say?"

"This isn't about me and you, Rich."

"You're right," T-Mac spoke up. He leaned forward, resting his folded arms atop the table. "It's about me since I'm the one who got popped that night. So, it should be my say so. And I say we off the nigga Coop. And if we find out Swindle lied, then we off his ass too."

"I'm with T-Mac on this," Danger said. He passed the blunt to T-Mac.

"So am I," C-Note second.

"You two with me?" T-Mac asked both his cousins.

"Always," Rich agreed.

"Fa sho," Don assured.

T-Mac leaned back in his seat and blew weed smoke into the air. "Then we'll get at that nigga Coop ASAP. And if Swindle lyin', then he dyin'."

"Don't trip. Eventually, we'll get at them any-fuckin'-way in order to take over the hood," Danger said.

"On the real, we need to get at them niggas ASAP 'cause they're gettin' in the way of us makin' more paper," C-Note added.

"I'ont want beef gettin' in the way of us gettin' money, but I ain't lettin' the beef slide with whoever popped me," T-Mac made plain.

"And neither are we. But first, we need to find out exactly who it was. Until then, let's stay focused on chasin' a check," Rich told him.

Don poured up the bottle to his lips. "Look, it's too much ass and titties in here to be talkin' about some beef and money shit right now. For the night, let's just ball out." He called over the stripper, who was the main attraction at the club named Mahogany. She sashayed over to their table wearing a long blond wig and leopard lingerie with gold stilettos. "Boo, why don't you take my nigga here back into the champaign room and give him a private dance? Careful, he's a l'il fragile right now."

Mahogany took T-Mac by the hand and led him towards one of the private rooms. Don and Rich and C-Note and Danger all remained in the VIP section, poppin' bottles and showering strippers with money. For the remainder of the night, the crew allowed themselves to take their minds off the blood money and bloody murder awaiting them in the streets.

CHAPTER 15

"Rob, we can't have any more close calls like that. If so, then either he goes, or I go."

"I won't have any of that. You just leave him to me; I'll be sure to talk with him about it."

TJ ended his call with Rob. He was still heated at Bone over the close call during their last lick. Kayla entered the living room and made her way over to TJ, who was seated on the couch. She knew that whenever he sat around with no electronics on, then something was on his mind.

"What's on your mind?" Kayla asked as she sat on the couch beside him.

"It's nothin'." TJ took a swig of his drink.

Kayla grabbed his hand in hers. "TJ, I know you well enough to know when something's on your mind. What is it, baby?"

TJ let out a forced breath. "Just shit that has to do with Bone."

"I should've known," Kayla replied. "And what about him?"

"It's just that I'ont much trust his intentions. But Rob don't seem to see anything wrong dealin' with Bone."

"Maybe there isn't anything wrong with it."

TJ cut his eyes at her and said, "Not you too." He shook his head.

"I'm just saying that maybe you should try seeing things with Bone differently. He has been your homeboy far before I came into the picture. And before then, you two were close," Kayla expounded.

"Me not trustin' Bone has nothin' to do with you. How can I trust in a nigga who put my fuckin' life in jeopardy?"

"The same way you did for so long," she answered his rhetorical question.

TJ knew she had a point. "Kayla, do you still have any feelings for Bone?"

This question took Kayla by surprise. "What? No, I don't. Look, what Bone and I had was nothing close to what you and I have, TJ. And I only want you," she told him. "It's no secret that I used to have feelings for Bone, but that was before you and I got together. Now my feelings are wrapped up in you, TJ." She went to give TJ a kiss on the lips, and he turned his head, offering his cheek.

"If you say so, Kayla." TJ withdrew his hand. He then said, "Look, I need to go and clear my headspace."

After collecting his keys and gun, TJ headed out the door. Kayla didn't even attempt to stop him from leaving because she figured he needed a moment. She just watched from the window as TJ stepped into his Audi truck and then zoomed down the street. TJ was on his way to the pool hall in order to have himself a couple of drinks.

•••

Swindle was seated at the bar in the pool hall. He took a swig of his drink while thoughts of how shit in the streets was going slid through his mind. He felt Heavy was letting Don get away with testing his savage, without Don even knowing about it.

His attention was grabbed by some commotion near a pool table. Looking over, he noticed there was Bone staring down the barrel of the gun.

"Look, that's all the money I have on me. I'll get you the rest," Bone said pleadingly.

"Youngsta, you have some nerve comin' in here and gamblin' with your life! You still owe me eight-grand, and I want every damn penny of it!" the O.G. cat named Benny asserted. He pressed the muzzle of his snub nose .357 revolver to Bone's jaw and hissed, "Since you didn't have all my goddamn cash upfront, now I want double the ten grand you bet and loss. Or you can pay with your life."

"A'ight, a'ight. Benny, I'll get you your paper just as soon as I get ahold of it."

"And when you get my cash, then you know where to find me." Benny replaced the gun on his hip.

Being in the game a long time, Benny was in his early sixties and had been through it all. He'd done fifteen years flat in federal prison for a slew of charges and had nearly been killed on a few occasions within his lifetime. He was light-skinned with freckles, hazel eyes, a frail build, a long, salt and pepper slicked-back ponytail, and could pass to be at least ten years younger than his actual age. Benny was an O.G. who had clout in the game. So, it wouldn't be shit for him to get a nigga knocked off. Bone made his way out of the pool hall. His first thought was to kill Benny whenever he got the chance. Instead, he would have to find a way to get the cash and pay off Benny, although, in the end, Bone planned to give Benny what he had coming.

"Yo Bone," Swindle called after him as Bone reached his car. After overhearing what took place inside the pool hall, Swindle seen this as the perfect opportunity to make a move. "I need to rap with you a minute."

"I'ont have time for it," Bone told him as he pulled open the driver's door.

"Then maybe you should make time for it if you wanna get paid."

Bone looked to him with a quirked brow and asked, "How can I get paid fuckin' with you, Swindle?"

"Same way you and your gang been gettin' paid. I got a lick on deck for you."

"And why put me up on a lick? What's in it for you?" Curious.

"Figure we can benefit from each other on this. Bone, I overhead what took place in there with Benny. And we both know you need some paper to pay up, or else."

"Look, I'll pay Benny's monkey-ass when I feel like it." Attitude.

Swindle shook his damn head. "I advise you to take me up on my offer. That way, we both can get what we need in the end. All you have to do is lay down this nigga and get him out the way, then sell his work to us. You know, the usual. And once you get paid, then you'll be able to pay off your debt with Benny," Swindle laid out.

Bone weighed his options for a brief moment. "Look, maybe if I get desperate, then I'll consider takin' your offer. I'll find a way to pay Benny, even if I have to pay him in blood."

"Just remember that money is cheaper than blood," Swindle told him.

Bone stepped into his car, brought the engine to life then sped away. He had to admit that Swindle's offer was tempting, but he didn't exactly know Swindle's angle. Bone just had to find a way to get the twenty G's owed to Benny. Swindle's right. I can use the money, Bone reconsidered mentally. He spun the car around the block and parked outside the pool hall. Then he stepped out and headed back for the pool hall in search of Swindle. Entering the pool hall, Bone spotted Swindle sitting at the bar. He figured he'd find Swindle there. After his debt with Benny, he reconsidered

Swindle's offer and wanted to take him up on it. Bone desperately needed to pay the debt owed as soon as possible if he didn't want to have Benny send shooters for him. Although, he plotted to make Benny pay him back.

Bone slid onto the barstool beside Swindle and said, "A'ight, I'm in."

"Guess desperate times calls for desperate measures," Swindle jabbed and then took a swig from his bottle of Budweiser. He gestured for the barkeeper to bring over Bone a Budweiser on him. "Figured you'd reconsider takin' my offer. Never met a jack-boy who turned down a sweet lick."

"Well, here I am. Now, who's this nigga you got in mind to be laid down?"

Swindle shifted towards him on the stool. "The nigga's name is Don. He's pushin' weight in the game, so you're bound to come up off his ass. I'll tell you where to find him, but it's in you to do your homework on the nigga. Once you and your gang lay him down, then Heavy and I will cash out for whatever work you come up with. Business as usual. Just make sure you get the job done."

"Done deal," Bone assured.

"And let's keep this between us."

Swindle knew that he could use Bone to get rid of Don because he was sure Bone and his gang would murk the nigga. It was a perfect setup for Swindle. He would get rid of Don without getting his hands dirty, and buying the work would be a consolation. The way Swindle saw it, he was doing the dirty work for Heavy. It was the way they would stay on top in this dirty game.

Leaving Swindle to his drink, Bone slid off the stool and made his exit. Unbeknownst to Bone, TJ had entered the pool hall while Bone had spun the block before returning. TJ had taken up a secluded booth near the back, and he observed Bone and Swindle's intense conclave.

Sipping at his glass of 1942, TJ wondered, *What the fuck could Bone and Swindle be up to?*

•••

It was nearly midnight when Coop stumbled out of the gamble spot wasted. Ever since his right-hand man Trip had been smoked, gambling and drinking were how he mourned. He'd been kicked out of the spot after he became belligerent over losing damn near three bands on craps. Now he was about to head to the pool hall.

Coop staggered his way through the darkened gangway towards the front street where his car was parked. He didn't expect Rich and T-Mac to be posted up in the gangway. They'd gotten word from a nigga in their gang that Coop was inside. While Rich was on the lookout, Tay-Mac pulled his Glock and snatched up Coop by the shirt, then forced him back up against the house.

"Fuck's goin' on?!" Coop wanted to know.

"Word is you had somethin' to do with airin' out our trap," T-Mac growled.

"Dawg, I ain't have shit to do with that! Whoever told you that is a lyin' muthafucka!"

"Of course, you gon' say that with this pole in your face. You a killa, right? Then don't switch up now."

"Why in the fuck would I air out y'all niggas?"

"'Cause you know that after we found out y'all was pushin' work on the side, we murked ya boy, Trip."

Coop looked perplexed. "I shoulda known it was y'all niggas all along instead of Swindle," he cried.

"So, you mean to tell me that you didn't know we offed Trip?" T-Mac asked.

"Not until now. But it makes sense bein' that y'all tryna take over the hood on Heavy and Swindle. The fucked-up thing is that neither side gives a fuck about who y'all gotta takeout to do so," Coop uttered.

"You right." T-Mac struck Coop upside the head with the gun causing him to crumple onto the ground, and then T-Mac stood abroad him and squeezed the trigger twice.

Boc! Boc!

The flashes from the muzzle lit up the gangway. One slug hit Coop in the chest at point-blank range, and the second landed in his neck. Coop died on impact. T-Mac and Rich left Coop dead in the gangway. However, T-Mac knew he couldn't just leave Coop alive now that Coop was aware that they had whacked Trip, knowing that Coop was bound to avenge his boy. T-Mac now understood that Swindle was playing them, and he wanted him dead.

As they slid through traffic, Rich noticed T-Mac seemed off. "Thought you'd be satisfied after doin' Coop back there."

"I would be if it was Coop who was the nigga who aired out our trap," T-Mac replied.

"What you mean it wasn't Coop?"

T-Mac shifted towards him. "When I brought up us smokin' Trip, Coop mentioned he thought it was Swindle who did it."

"Then why did you off Coop?"

"'Cause I didn't want him comin' for us after tellin' him we smoked Trip."

Rich pulled the whip to a stop at the stoplight. "So, you mean to tell me that Swindle misled us."

"That's my guess. And I'm sure it's because his ass had somethin' to do with our trap gettin' shot up."

"Look, don't trip. We'll let Swindle think we don't know shit and wait for the right time to hit up him and Heavy."

Rich knew they had to tie up all loose ends, and T-Mac was all for it.

CHAPTER 16

"Hell are you doin' here?" Rob asked. Once he answered the knock on his loft door, he found Bone.

"Take a ride with me," Bone insisted. Reluctantly Rob decided to ride along with Bone in order to see what he had in mind. Through the night streets, Bone pushed his blue Yukon Denali with Rob seated on his right. Rob had no idea where Bone was taking him, being that Bone had dropped by his place unannounced and insisted Bone take a ride with him without offering many details. Rob was curious as to where Bone insisted on taking him. They rode in silence as Icewear Vezzo's "The Lick" played in the background.

Bone pulled the Yukon to a stop at a stoplight and lowered the volume on the music, then said, "I 'preciate you ridin' with me."

"It's the least I can do for you after what you did for me and the others," Rob replied. He peered over at Bone, then added, "I 'preciate that far more."

"Don't mention it, Rob. I only did what any of you woulda done if the roles were reversed. The only thing I can't wrap my head around is how come Max visited regularly, but you never came to visit once. I can understand why TJ didn't, bein' that he wasn't real enough to look me in the eyes and tell me about him and Kayla." Bone snorted. He met Rob's eyes. "But why didn't you pay me a visit, Rob?"

Rob peered out the passenger window at the passing traffic. "Bone, I just felt it was best that I didn't give the investigators any reason to link me to the case." He found Bone's eyes and added: "Besides, I didn't wanna see you on lockdown. And I had a feelin' that you would beat the case and return to the gang."

"Yeah, well, it seems like not everyone gives a fuck about my return."

"Look, I'm sure you mean TJ. I'll admit that him gettin' with Kayla isn't cool, but I'm sure it was nothin' he intended to happen. You and TJ need to rap. He may seem like he doesn't give a fuck, but he does."

"If TJ wants to rap, then we can. But I ain't tryna hear shit he has to say about that lick in the past."

"Bone, you can't blame TJ for feelin' a way about that lick when you went outside of the game plan and not only nearly got us all booked but also nearly smoked."

Bone snorted and shifted towards him. "Yeah, but it didn't happen that way 'cause I was the one who caught a bullet and a body for all of you. And I kept it solid and didn't speak about that body like a real one. So, all due respect, I'ont wanna hear shit else about that lick," he asserted.

"I can respect that, Bone. As long as you don't make that same error again. I just need you to understand that there's no room for errors because next time, it could turn out for the worst for all of us. A'ight." Rob knew it was best not to take sides.

"Rob, I had three years on lockdown to think about that error. So that's the last thing you gotta worry about with me," Bone assured. He pulled off with traffic when the light flipped green.

En route, Bone and Rob stopped to also pick up Max and then TJ. Now that the gang was all together, they headed towards the destination.

"Hell are we goin'?" TJ pressed.

"Don't worry, TJ, no one is kidnappin' you," Bone jeered.

Max took a pull on his square then said, "Can we at least know what's goin' on."

"Why don't you two just wait and see because the only one who knows a thing is Bone. So, let's trust in him," Rob told them.

TJ scoffed at the idea of putting trust in Bone.

"Problem with what Rob said?" Bone questioned, glancing at TJ through the rearview mirror.

"No, he doesn't have a problem with it. Right, TJ?" Max intervened, cutting his eyes over at TJ.

"Yeah, right." TJ shook his damn head.

Shortly thereafter, Bone pulled to the curb and parked down the street from a trap house with the red Range Rover parked out front. This trap belonged to Don and his gang, and Bone had been staking it out for a couple of days now. Don stood on the front porch of the trap along with C-Note and Danger, each oblivious to the jack boy's observation from down the street.

"This is what I brought you all to check out." Bone pointed out the trap house.

"You want us to lay down a trap," Rob said.

"Not exactly. I want us to lay down the nigga who runs the trap. Name's Don, and from what I gather, the nigga is holdin'."

"And how'd you come upon this lick?"

"The question is when will we hit this lick," Bone deflected, answering Rob's question and not mentioning Swindle.

"If we're gonna hit this lick, then we're gonna do it my way," Rob insisted.

"Then have it your way," Bone agreed.

"We'll catch that nigga when he least expects it and then murk his ass."

"Say no more."

Bone didn't want Rob knowing he and Swindle had made a deal behind his back in order to prevent Rob from turning down the lick. Bone needed to hit this lick in order to come upon enough bread to payoff Benny, which was something else he wouldn't tell Rob. He was sure that Rob would have something to say about his gambling habit, so Bone rather keep as many details to himself as he could. The main thing that mattered is the lick.

On the other hand, Rob was a bit skeptical of this particular lick. Mainly because Bone wasn't usually one to come up with licks; instead, he just had his gun ready whenever a lick was on deck. Therefore, Rob figured there had to be a hidden agenda for Bone. But what? It wasn't so much that he didn't trust Bone. It was that he didn't know what Bone was capable of. However, Rob wasn't against hittin' the lick.

Bone smirked as they rode off down the street past Don, who was unaware that he was next up on the gang's list to be murked.

•••

After making a quick stop at the trap spot to pick up some work, Don went on his way with Shanta riding beside him in the passenger seat of the Range. At times he would bring his girl along when he was trappin', and she didn't mind because she knew it was how he provided for them. In fact, Shanta played her role as Don's trap queen. She often held his sack and pole while in traffic. Don never cared to put her in harm's way.

Meeting up with his clientele, Juice, at their usual spot, Don pulled into the parking lot of Popeye's. He grabbed the half of key from Shanta before stepping out of the Range. After making the drug deal with Juice, Don entered the whip and pushed on. Shanta shifted towards Don in her seat. "Don, you know I'll do anything for you," she told him.

"No doubt. And I'll do the same for you," Don replied, keeping his eyes on traffic.

"I respect how you provide for us, although do you plan on ever getting out the game?"

He glanced over at her. "Now you're startin' to sound just like my moms with that shit. Shan, I'm doin' what I have to."

"I just want to see you do something different."

"So does my moms." Don snorted. He understood his mom and girl's concerns, although he was in too deep.

"I'm sure she does. By the way, how is she?"

"She's much better after rehab. Now she just has to stay clean." Don braked to a stop at a stoplight. "Listen, the game is the reason I was able to get my moms out of the hood and provide for you. So, I respect whatever comes with the game."

Don pulled his Range to the curb before Pak's jewelry shop. Now that his money was right, he wanted to cop some jewels to go along with it. He hopped out the whip, followed by Shanta. They approached the establishment and had to be buzzed in. Inside, Don made his way up to the glass showcase and checked out a few pieces. Shortly thereafter, Geno, the jeweler, approached.

"What can I help you with?"

"I need them right there," Don said, pointing out a pair of 1.25 karats diamond earrings with yellow-gold trim.

"Good taste in jewelry, I see."

"How much?"

"For you today, $500. Anything else I can help you with?"

"I need a chain to match them boogers. Nothin' too major, though."

"I have just what you need." The jeweler came out of the showcase with a yellow-gold Cuban link necklace. "This will set you back $1,950."

"Cool."

"Anything else?"

"Yeah. I'd like the Rolex that my girl keeps eyein'." Don smirked at Shanta. She didn't even realize he had noticed, and her face lit up with surprise.

"Nice choice," Geno, the jeweler, smiled as he reached inside the showcase for the lady Rolex. It was plain-Jain, dipped in yellow-gold.

"And lemme get the identical one there," Don referred to the Rolex for men, wanting them to have matching his and hers timepieces.

"I'll give you both for $7,200 flat."

"Box 'em up!"

"That'll be $9,650 in total, plus tax." The jeweler rang up the jewels and then placed the items along with jewelry rags and wipes, and cleaners into a bag. Don pulled out a bankroll, peeled off the total, and cashed out, then he signed his receipts and gave the jeweler his name to log into the file. "You're all set to go," Geno, the jeweler, said.

Don, along with Shanta, exited Pak's jewelry shop. He failed to realize that diamonds and gold couldn't cover his scars.

•••

Bone hit the blunt before passing it to his right to Max. The two were seated on the bleachers in the park. It was a night out, and they were the only ones there, aside from some juvenile delinquents. Bone and Max were close, so they could often be found together.

"So, when will we lay down this nigga Don?" Max wanted to know. He hit the blunt.

"Whenever Rob thinks it's best," Bone said. "This is my lick so, why should we have to wait on Rob's say so? If you ask me, we should go and hit the lick tonight. The sooner, the better."

Max looked over at him. "But you know Rob wants to make sure shit checks out."

Bone snorted. "Rob just wants to be in charge all of the damn time. Don't you ever wanna take charge, Max? It doesn't always have to be Rob's way. I know that nigga ain't in charge of me."

"I'm sure it ain't even like that. Rob just wants to look out for our best interest."

"Then how come when I ended up on lockdown fighting for my damn freedom, not one time did he look out for me?!" Bone spat. He felt like he had been left to fend for himself, and over time it made him bitter. "Not to mention that nigga, TJ, did me wrong. How could he get with Kayla behind my back like it wasn't shit?" Bone shook his fuckin' head.

Max could see why Bone was bitter. "Look, if you ask me, Rob should have done more for you while you were on lockdown. However, he did acknowledge you keepin' it solid. As for TJ, I can't speak for him but, I'm sure he doesn't feel good about gettin' with Kayla the way he did. Besides, you and her were hardly together, so you shouldn't be offended."

"Max, do you really think Rob givin' me acknowledgement was enough when I had to sit three years in jail, not knowing if I'd ever see the streets again? He owes me more than that. He couldn't even pay me a fuckin' visit. And TJ, his ass, knew how I felt about Kayla. But he can have her 'cause payback is a bitch. But you kept it real with me. So, you're the main one that I trust with my life, Max. The only thing is I ain't afraid to lose my life." Bone looked him dead in the eyes.

"Not only me but Rob and TJ will never put your life in danger, Bone. And I'm sure we can trust you with our lives in your hands. It's been that way for half our lives," Max told him.

Bone shifted towards him and stated, "Let's just hope they don't put *their* lives at risk." He grabbed the blunt from Max and took a pull of the exotic weed.

After leaving the park, Bone slid through traffic on the way to drop off Max. During the ride, Max's mind was jumbled. He understood that Bone was bitter, but he didn't know if that would affect the gang. Max just hoped that once they got back to hittin' licks, then the gang would be as tight as it was before.

Bone pulled to a stop before Max's place. The two shook up, and then as Max was finna step out, Bone said, "Think about yourself for once, and stop lettin' Rob think for you all of the damn time Max."

"Then I think you and Rob should really figure shit out," Max replied.

"I figure it is what it is. Anyways, have your gun ready to hit the lick on that nigga, Don." Bone pulled off down the street, leaving Max with that thought.

•••

While at TJ's crib, he and Rob were in the front room seated on the couch, sharing a blunt of loud with a Milwaukee Brewers game on TV. Rob had stopped by to see where TJ's head was at surrounding all that was going on because he had noticed that lately, TJ hadn't seemed to have a clear head. And in this game, if a nigga didn't have his head on right, then he could lose it.

TJ sipped the bottle of 1942 and then passed it to his nigga. "The thing I like most about the game of baseball is stealing bases. Because if the player isn't fast enough and don't know the right time to make a steal, then he'll be caught slidin' home and get dugout," he analogized.

"Sounds a lot like the game we're in. The difference is, if we get three strikes, then we're out of the game for good," Rob compared. He hit the bottle.

"Which is why in this game, we gotta play our positions the right way."

Rob eyed him observantly. "And that means havin' your head in the game. Lately, yours haven't seemed to be there. What's that about, TJ?"

"It's just all of the shit that's been taking place ever since Bone got back into the game with us. I'ont trust the nigga like I once used to."

"So, what's your take on the lick Bone has set up?"

"I take it he's usin' our guns to his advantage. Who knows how he even came across this lick? Rob, if you're in, then so am I," TJ said.

"Well, I'm all in."

"Then just get at me with the details."

"Say no more."

TJ leaned back in his seat. "For whatever it's worth, the other day I saw Bone rappin' with that nigga Swindle at the pool hall, and it looked intense." He felt the need to bring this to Rob's attention.

"I must admit that I'ont trust Swindle, although they coulda been rappin' about anything," Rob replied, giving Bone the benefit of doubt. He sipped from the bottle. "I still got Swindle's chain, just in case I need it as an incentive."

"An incentive?"

Rob met his eyes. "Right. Just in case I need to reel his ass in for any reason."

With a plate of hot wings in hand, Kayla entered the front room. She set the plate on the coffee table for the boys.

Without being told, Kayla knew how to cater to her man. Keeping TJ satisfied was all she wanted, and he did his all to keep her happy. Though their relationship made them feel like they wronged Bone, for them, being together felt right.

"Good lookin', baby," TJ told Kayla and smacked her ass as she went on her way.

"Sure, she don't have a part in why you don't trust Bone so much anymore?" Rob wanted to know.

TJ grabbed up a wing and took a bite. "All I'll say is that I trust Kayla over him."

"Look, we've never had a reason not to trust Bone before. So, let's give him the benefit of doubt."

"And what if he gives us a reason over some fuckin' money, Rob?"

Rob turned up the bottle to his lips and then used his backhand to wipe away liquor trekking down his chin. "Then I'll bury him with it," he solemnly swore. TJ could read that he was dead serious. Rob set the bottle on the table, then stood and said, "I got someplace to be. I'll get with you." He left out on his way, leaving TJ to his own thoughts.

Even though TJ had agreed to be in on the lick that Bone came upon, he still had his own personal reservations. TJ didn't want shit to be personal with him and Bone. Although he knew how shit went between them, which also involved Kayla made it just that much more complicated. Aside from that, TJ didn't much trust Bone's intentions.

Riding to YNW Melly's "Thugged Out", Rob's thoughts drifted into the air. He couldn't help but think about what he and TJ had discussed pertaining to Bone. Just because he trusted TJ didn't mean he didn't trust Bone. One thing for sure and two things for certain, Rob trusted none when it comes to his money.

Martell "Troublesome" Bolden

CHAPTER 17

"Don't worry, you look beautiful," Rich comforted Brittany. He readjusted the front of her black strapless Versace dress. "Better." They were at Angie's home, where she was serving her usual Sunday dinner. Brittany didn't know what to expect during her first time meeting Angie. She just hoped that Angie was as nice as Rich made her out to be.

"But what if she doesn't like me?" Brittany worried.

"She will. I already told her all about you."

"Like what?"

"All good things, of course. Just be yourself, and you'll be okay. Now c'mon." He took Brittany by her manicured hand and led her inside his mother's home.

The aroma of food wafted throughout the home. Rich and Brittany entered the dining room, finding the table set beautifully and dressed with pots, platters, and pans of different foods. And already seated at the table was Don beside Shanta.

"Was beginnin' to think you wouldn't show, Rich," Don sniped.

"Don, I'm here for mama," Rich told him.

Don snorted. "Where were you when she needed you most?"

"Don, please stop," Shanta piped in and nudged him. "Anyway. Glad you two could make it."

"Thanks, Shanta. Nice to see you again," Brittany spoke up.

Rich said, "And Shanta, I'm glad that you're here at least." He heard pots and pans banging in the kitchen. "Mama, we're here," he called out.

"I'll be there in a moment," Angie called back. She came into the dining room from the kitchen carrying a dish of mac

& cheese. At first sight of Brittany, she stopped in her tracks. Angie couldn't believe how gorgeous she was.

"Mama, this is my girl, Brittany," Rich introduced them.

"Pleased to meet you," Brittany smiled.

Angie set the dish atop the table before stepping over to Brittany. She gently planted a hand on Brittany's cheek and, with a smile, said, "You're even more beautiful than Richard described."

"Thanks, Ms. Angie."

"Please, just call me Angie. Why don't you have a seat," she offered. "Don and Rich, be nice enough to grab the last of the dishes from the kitchen, will you?"

Don stood and then headed for the kitchen. Rich pulled out chairs at the table for both Angie and Brittany, and they took a seat before he turned for the kitchen as well, leaving the women alone.

"Brittany, I want you to know that Rich really likes you. A woman has never made him happier before, including myself. And I'm sure you like him more than he knows," Angie said.

"Ms. Ang—. Sorry. Angie, I don't mean to get in the way of how he feels about you. And yes, I do like Rich, maybe more than he knows. I have hopes for the future for him and me," Brittany expounded.

"And I'm sure he's hopeful also," Angie smiled. She looked into the faces of both Shanta and Brittany, then added, "My boys are fortunate to have good women like you two in their lives."

Carrying dishes of food, Don and Rich returned to the dining room, where they placed the dishes atop the table among the others. They then took their seats at the table, Don beside Shanta and Rich beside Brittany. Angie was seated at the head of the table.

"Hope you girls are gettin' along," Don commented.

"We can say the same about you boys," Angie replied, looking from Don to Rich, feeling the tension.

"Let's just say there's brotherly love," Rich inserted.

"How about I say grace," Angie told them, and everyone bowed their heads. "God, thank you for bringing me closer to my sons. Only You know how much I love them. And thank You for blessing them both with good women. No matter what may family come first. Amen."

After Angie's grace, the others murmured "Amen" around the table. Don and Rich both knew the grace was meant for them.

During dinner, Angie noticed her boys were unusually quiet and stared daggers at each other over the table. She understood that apparently, they still had differences. After dinner, the girls offered to help Angie with the dishes. Angie found Don and Rich in the front room and took it upon herself to try and mend things between them.

"Don, Rich," Angie began as she made her way over towards the mantle, where she took a look at a photo of the two together as kids. "It's obvious the two of you are beefing, and I don't like it. So, whatever it is, y'all need to figure it out. Because I won't sit back and let y'all be this way towards each other." She looked from one to the other and added, "No matter what, you should always be your brother's keeper." Leaving them with that thought, Angie headed back into the kitchen with the girls.

Don shifted towards Rich and said, "L'il bro, mom's right. It doesn't have to be this way between us."

"It's your fault that it is," Rich stated.

"What do you want from me, Rich? Huh?"

"Don, I want you to stop drawing so much attention to us with all of your jewels, whips, and shit. That way, we don't have to worry about dodgin' bullets and indictments."

"So be it. No matter what, we can't prevent bullets or indictments from comin' our way. That's just part of the game," Don expounded.

"Listen, I just don't want anything to happen to you."

"Rich, we gotta be willin' to accept whatever happens in this game. Although, I give my word that I won't let shit happen to me or you without goin' all-out," Don vowed.

"Same," Rich swore.

The brothers were able to put aside their differences. Don understood Rich just wanted him to be at his best. And Rich was down for Don no matter what. They wouldn't let the power of money come between them. With all that was going on behind their backs, they needed to have each other's backs in the game.

•••

Rich shifted the Lexus through traffic as Brittany puffed on the blunt of za-za while riding in the passenger seat. It being later in the evening, the sky was a dark pink as the sun sank on the horizon.

"My moms seem to really take a likin' to you," Rich commented.

"And I like her, too. She's a good person," Brittany replied. She pulled on the weed once more before passing the blunt to Rich. "After meeting Angie, I just don't get why you held any ill feelings towards her."

"You don't know her very well. My ma wasn't always such a good person. She was an addict and didn't seem to give a damn about my bro or me." He hit the blunt.

"Rich, don't speak like that about your mom. Apparently, she does care. Because despite her past, she's now there for you and Don," she told him.

"Yeah, you right." He braked at the red light and then puffed the blunt. "Look, I'm glad that I have you. Never did a nigga imagine havin' a girl that makes me better. But then you came along and redesigned my imagination. I just wish it woulda been sooner."

"Well, you have me now, Rich. And I'm all yours, as long as you continue to appreciate me."

"Then I'll treat you better than better as a token of my appreciation," he replied solemnly, peering into Brittany's eyes.

"Listen..." She placed a hand on his thigh in comfort. "You caring about me is all I need to feel appreciated. Just know that I'm all you need."

"Likewise."

Arriving at Brittany's apartment complex in the suburbs, Rich veered the whip to the curb out front. She pecked his lips and then said, "Call me as soon as you get home, so I know that you're safe."

"Will do."

"And maybe you should give your brother a call also. Believe it or not, tonight I seen the brotherly love between you and Don."

Rich smirked. "Don knows I love his ass, even when he's trippin'."

Brittany shook her head. "Boy, just call once you get home, alright?" She stepped out of the car and headed for the building. Once she entered, then Rich pulled off.

As Rich slid through the night traffic, Moneybagg Yo's tune "Change Da Subject" played at a lowered volume in the background. His thoughts drifted into the air along with the weed smoke. Brittany was still on his mind; he couldn't help but think of what she had said about his mother being there for him and Don after all. Brittany's right, he contemplated. I need to see the good in moms. And as for Don, damn, maybe I should give his ass a call like Brittany suggested. Rich had to admit that Brittany made him want to be better and do better.

His thoughts were interrupted once noticing the silver SUV up ahead in traffic which was used by the shooters during the night. Rich and his gang were targeted at the trap spot. He already had an idea of who had a part in the shooting, but he didn't know exactly who the shooters were. So, gettin' at the niggas in the SUV would have to satisfy his thirst for retaliation for now.

The SUV yielded to a halt at a stoplight. Gripping the Glock .45 with a thirty-shot stick, Rich slid the Lexus beside the passenger side of the SUV. Due to its tinted windows, he couldn't get a good look at any of the niggas inside but was sure they were the shooters. Aiming the gun out the window at the SUV, Rich opened fire.

Boc-Boc-Boc,-Boc!

Bullets decorated the SUV with holes and shattered its windows, and some struck the driver in the chest twice and the passenger in the shoulder. The driver mustered enough strength to smash off through bypassing traffic cutting off vehicles and causing motorists to blow their horns in protest. Giving chase, Rich zipped through traffic behind the weaving SUV. Approximately a block later, the SUV veered uncontrollably into a tree at high speed and crashed hard. The passenger bailed out of the totaled SUV and fled in between two buildings. Rich braked his whip in the street near the crashed SUV and hopped out with his gun in hand, then stepped over to the driver's side of the SUV finding the driver slumped on his side and fighting for his breath.

"Who sent you niggas at us that night?" Rich demanded. He didn't recognize the driver at all and didn't get a good look at the fleeing passenger.

"I-I'm... already about to d-die... So, I ain't s-sayin' s-shit..." the driver managed to say. He began gasping for air. Rich pressed the muzzle of the .45 to his top, then stated, "Say no more."

Boc!

After splattering the driver's brains all over the dashboard, Rich jumped back into the Lexus and murked off down the street. He didn't gather who put the hit out on them to be sure of it, although he had no doubt about who came to mind. Rich just wanted to get the assailants before they could get him or any others in his gang.

Making it to his apartment complex Rich circled the block thrice while perpetually checking his rearview, finding no tail. Feeling comfortable enough to park, he pulled curbside out front of the complex. He rested his head back against the headrest and let out a deep breath. Grabbing up his iPhone from the cupholder, he called Don.

"S'up?" Don answered neutrally.

"Just want you to know that I'm down to ride or die for you," Rich told him.

"Say less. Feeling's mutual." Don understood that his l'il bro had rode out for him.

"I know."

After ending their call, Rich made his way into the complex and then to his apartment. Inside, he made his way to his bedroom, where he placed his .45 on the nightstand then kicked off his Balenciaga sneakers before jumping into the king-size bed. He pulled out his iPhone from the pocket of his Gucci denim jeans and called Brittany via FaceTime.

"Good to know you made it home safe," Brittany answered. She was also lying in bed after showering.

"Better safe than sorry." Rich smiled at her as though he didn't just commit murder.

•••

While a bad l'il bitch danced on top of the pool table to the music, Heavy sat on a stool at the wet bar, watching her clap her ass. She looked down into Heavy's eyes as she moved her body like a snake. Swindle entered the basement area of the spot while talking into his iPhone as the bitch continued her striptease for Heavy.

"Look, don't worry about that nigga. He'll be taken care of," Swindle told the caller on the other end of the phone before hanging up. He stepped over to the wet bar and grabbed a near-empty bottle of Remy, then turned it up to his lips. Sitting on the vacant stool beside Heavy, Swindle breathed, "You ain't gonna believe this shit."

"What is it?" Heavy asked, never taking his eyes off the bitch.

"It's Rich. The nigga slid on Q and Vito in traffic and fanned 'em out."

"They good?"

"That was just Vito on the phone. Said Q's dead," Swindle informed. He took a gulp of the liquor.

Heavy finally removed his eyes from the bitch, setting them on Swindle. "We gonna have to dead Rich ass, too, if we don't want the nigga to retaliate after we hit Don," he urged.

"Say no more. Dead men can't retaliate."

CHAPTER 18

"Mmm, yes, baby, it feels so damn good!" Trina moaned erotically while she rode Rob's dick. As she grinded on him, her titties jiggled. Leaning forward, Trina gently bit Rob's lower lip. Her body began to quiver, and her moans grew louder as a wave of orgasm took its course.

Palming her juicy ass in both hands, Rob slammed Trina up and down on his stiff dick, sliding deep inside her slippery slit. A nut swelled up in the tip of cock. "Damn, boo!" Rob grunted as he busted a nut.

Trina rolled beside Rob in bed, and the two were covered in perspiration, panting from their good fuckin'. Since Rob didn't care to have her over to his place, she had called him over to hers so they could suck and fuck. With the understanding that they weren't together exclusively, Trina had hope for her and Rob. Although, she knew that he wasn't much of a hopeless romantic.

"Been thinkin' about the mark you brought to my attention. Has his bitch happened to say anything else about the nigga?" Rob wanted to know.

"Not much... just... what I already... told you," Trina answered in between, planting kisses on his neck.

"No name of his, no hood he be in, no whip he pushes," he pressed, wanting to know something about the mark.

She halted her kisses and met his eyes. "Rob, I already told you everything I know so far. Once the bitch comes in again, then I'll try getting details on her nigga, alright."

"A'ight, Trina. Just make sure your ass gets as many details as you can outta the bitch on the nigga." His tone was direct.

"And I will. Just gimme some time," Trina told him. She rested her head on his chest. "Rob, if you don't mind me asking, what would you do with yourself if you weren't robbing?"

"Why ask?"

"Because I would just like to know."

Rob understood that she cared to know more about him, but he'd rather not open up much at all to her because, for him, it was nothing personal. "Just know that I'ma mask up, rob, and kill until I hit a lick that will change my life. So hopefully, the mark you brought to my attention will do just that," was all he said.

While the two lay in silence, Rob pondered long and hard on Trina's question. He pondered on his answer even more. Like every jack-boy, Rob wanted a lick that would be a life-changer. But most ended up seeing life flash before their eyes.

•••

Parker turned down the quiet suburban street in her pearl white Mercedes-Benz GLA 250 SUV. The neighborhood was near the lakefront and was where some of the wealthiest resided. Most of the homes in the area were mini-mansions.

She'd just returned from Texas with a load on her way to drop it off to Castle. Castle used her as one of his road runners to traffic drugs and money wherever it needed to go. He really did like Parker, although she was more beneficial to him as a courier.

Arriving at her destination, Parker pulled into the drive-way of the huge, handsome home and parked behind a ruby red Bentley GT Continental. As she stepped out of the SUV, Castle emerged from the home and made his way towards her. He gave her a hug and a peck on the lips. Parker seemed to melt in his arms. He was everything she wanted in a man; he was fine, smart, havin' money, and a hood nigga.

"How was the trip?" Castle inquired.

"No trouble. Everything's there," Parker assured.

"Good girl."

Castle motioned for one of his boys, who entered the SUV then hit the brakes and the light switch, causing the trap compartment to open. Concealed inside the trap were twenty kilos of coke. Castle's boy collected the keys then hauled them inside the home.

Once Castle and Parker made their way inside, they were in the master bedroom where Castle was seated on the California king bed while on the phone discussing business as Parker was preparing to take a shower after her road trip. Castle couldn't help but to admire Parker's frame as she pulled off her body-hugging Prada jogger suit, and knowing he was watching, she did it slowly as if to give him a striptease. He decided to end his call.

"Bring yo' pretty-ass here," Castle told her. Parker ambled over to him in only her white lace bra and panties. He lay back, and she straddled him. He smirked and said, "Now, please me."

Parker didn't hesitate to pull his dick out of his Blue Bands Only jogger pants and then dive her head into his lap, taking his dick into her mouth. She sucked him like she wanted a reward for it. Her tongue slid up and down its shaft and then twirled around its tip. He began guiding her mouth up and down on his dick. She used one of her petite hands to jack his hardness and the other to fondle with his sac as she orally pleased him. It didn't take her long to make Castle bust a nut. Afterwards, Parker climbed in bed and positioned herself on all fours, and Castle knelt behind her, pushed her panties to the side, and slid his joint deep inside her snatch.

"Unhhh... mmm... Yes, Castle. Fuck this pussy. Fuck it!"
Parker groaned. She gripped the satin sheets while looking
back over her shoulder as he fucked her hard. And Castle
loved how pretty her ass was, he slipped a thumb in her
asshole, and she enjoyed the double penetration. "Oooh boy,
I feel it cummin..." Her pussy tightened around his dick as
she reached climax.

Following their quickie, Castle stepped out of bed, fixed
his clothes, and then grabbed his iPhone to make more
business calls. Parker stepped up to him.

"Castle... I want... you... to... meet my friends..." Parker
said in between kisses on his neck.

"Whenever you want, boo. How 'bout we have them over
for a dinner party," Castle suggested.

"Sounds good."

"Then it's settled. Now, let me go and take care of this
business."

Castle headed for the study where his boys were breaking
the keys down and stepping on them. Once they were
packaged, each one was stamped with a Libra logo as his
trademark. Castle preferred to remain elusive in the game in
order to last.

•••

In the small café, Shanta and Kat occupied a table while
awaiting a late Parker. Growing impatient, Shanta waved
over a waitress, and she and Kat made their orders, and
Shanta placed an order for Parker without her there. This was
the fifth time this month Parker was running late, and one
day she didn't even show up at all.

"Lately, Parker's ass has been either showing up late or leaving early," Shanta commented as she checked the time on her yellow-gold Rolex.

"Maybe she lost track of time, who knows," Kat said, giving Parker the benefit of doubt.

"Maybe." Shanta figured it was something else.

"There Parker is now." Kat pointed out the picture window of the café.

Parker stepped out of her brand-new Benz truck. It was a gift from Castle and an upgrade from the early model Toyota Camry she normally drove. She entered the café and made her way over towards her girls. "Hey, bitches!" Parker greeted them. She took a seat in the vacant chair and set her expensive white Italian leather Birkin handbag atop the table. "Did I miss anything?"

"Not much. We did place our orders already, though. But don't worry, I ordered your usual for you," Shanta answered, sounding annoyed.

"Girl, I am so sorry that I'm late again. It's just that since I been with Castle, he demands lots of my time and shit. Forgive me."

"If you ask me, the nigga has every right to demand so much of your time since he's apparently taking good care of you," Kat offered her input. "He has you riding in a Mercedes and carrying a Birkin bag. Yes bitch, I forgive you."

"I know, right?" Parker concurred. She looked to Shanta. "How about you, Shan?"

Shanta leaned back in her chair with her arms folded beneath her breasts. "Despite what Kat thinks, it's not all about what a nigga is doing for you. Does he care about you is what matters most. But that whip and bag is dope!" She smiled and high-fived her girl. "I forgive you, boo. Now, how are things with you and Castle?"

"Everything's perfect. Castle just knows how to treat me," Parker gushed.

"What about the dick? Is it big, is it good?" Kat pried.

Parker chuckled. "Yes, girl. It's big and good!"

"He's fine, having money, and knows how to fuck, girl. You better do whatever it takes to keep Castle."

"Believe me; I will." Parker was willing to do just about anything to keep Castle in her life more than she let on.

"Parker, just don't allow Castle to use you because you like him so much," Shanta advised.

"Look, anything I do for Castle is because I'm willing to, not because he's using me. Okay, Shan?" Parker replied defensively.

Shanta could read that Parker seemed defensive, which wasn't typically like her. "That's not how I meant it. Girl, you know I just want to see you happy." She reached over the table and grabbed her girl's hand, and added, "All that matters is that you're happy. If you're happy, then I'm happy for you. And I'm looking forward to getting to know Castle."

"Thanks, girl."

"Enough about that, let's talk about me," Kat half-joked, causing both Shanta and Parker to laugh.

The waitress returned with the table's orders. After servicing the girls, the waitress went on her way.

Shanta looked at her friends and said, "I'm glad you're my girls. Now, let's eat."

•••

In the kitchen of her home, Angie was standing at the stove cooking macaroni & cheese while the music played from Alexa. She was accompanied by Don, who set on a stool at the island. He had come by to give his mom some money for bills and decided to stay over for lunch. Angie knew mac & cheese was her boys' favorite food. Maybe that had to do with it being one of the only meals she could afford to feed them back in the days as kids. They had come a long way from those days.

Angie stirred the pot of macaroni. "Don, how's things been going with you and Shanta?" she wanted to know.

"She and I have been in a good place. There's somethin' about her that I just can't get enough of," Don answered.

"Shan is a good girl, and I like you being with her."

"Part of her reminds me of you in a way, Ma."

"I'm sure you aren't talking about her cooking," Angie half-joked.

Don chuckled, "Leave my baby alone. She'll never be able to cook like you." He rested his elbows atop the island. "Aside from that, Shanta is all I need."

"I'm glad that you and Rich have girls that mean so much to you. Now maybe one of you will give me a grand-baby soon." Angie served him a bowl of mac & cheese.

"Ma, I'd love to give you a grandchild. But I can't speak for Rich."

At that moment, Rich just so happened to enter the kitchen, and he asked, "What about me?"

"I'm glad you're here also. I was just telling your brother how I want you two to give me some grandkids," Angie replied. "Thought you'd be satisfied with us givin' you this house and car. And now you want grandchildren too," Rich half-joked. He stood beside his brother.

"Boy, what's the use of having this big house if I don't have anyone to share it with. It'd be better if I had some grandbabies running around here. No pressure, I'm just saying."

"And I hear you, Ma. But for now, I'll leave it to Don." Rich patted his brother's back, who was enjoying his mac & cheese. "Now, how about a plate of this good food?"

Angie made Rich a bowl, and he sat beside Don as he dug in. She couldn't remember the last time the two got along so well. Angie understood that she was the main reason why they hadn't seen eye to eye over the years, so she would do her all to keep them together.

"Donte, Richard," Angie began soberly, and both of her boys looked up at her. "It means everything to me that you two are close again. I don't ever again want to be the reason why you have any differences. No matter what, I love both of you just the same," she expressed as tears sheened her eyes.

Don stood from the stool and made his way around the island to comfort his mom. "Listen, Ma, don't fault yourself for none of what happened. If it weren't for you, then Rich and I wouldn't even be as close as we are. I appreciate you more than you know."

"So do I," Rich piped in. "Ma, I know that I haven't always been the best son to you, but I never cared to see you doin' bad. And thanks to Don, you're doin' good now. Which is one reason why he and I are so close because of you."

Angie felt warm inside, knowing that both of her boys loved her. "Just hearing your words means so much to me."

At that moment, Cupid's tune "Cupid Shuffle" played into the music rotation on Alexa.

"I know you love this song, so you gotta give me this dance," Don said as he took his mom's hand. They began dancing around the kitchen to the music while Rich cheered them on.

After a moment, Rich approached and said, "Mind if I cut in?" He then had a turn dancing with his mom once Don stepped back.

Angie was all smiles and laughs. She enjoyed the moment with her sons. Once the song came to an end, she pecked both of her sons on their cheeks. "I don't know what I'd do if I ever lose either of you. Make sure you stay safe in these streets."

Both Don and Rich knew that they had to do their all to keep from losing their lives in the streets because the streets were merciless.

Martell "Troublesome" Bolden

CHAPTER 19

Loading up guns while riding under the moon, Rob, Bone, Max, and TJ inconspicuously tailed their next mark through traffic; it was Don. There was no banter among them, no conversation at all as they rode in the black Lexus SUV. They were each masked up and prepared to murk for the money.

Don steered towards his destination, gripping the pole across his lap in his right hand while steering with the other, which had the Rolex wrapped around its wrist. Arriving at his destination Don turned his Range into the parking lot of Popeye's, where he parked beside a silver BMW 745li. He was there to make a sale. Both Don and his clientele, Juice, stepped out of their whips into the night air, each with tote bags in hand, which individually contained bricks of pure cocaine and stacks of dead presidents.

Suddenly Max braked the SUV behind both the Range and BMW, barricading the vehicles. As Rob, Bone, and TJ hopped out with guns in hand, both Don and his mans drew their own.

Boc, boc, boc, boc, boc, boc!

Boom, boom, boom, boom!

The dope-boys and jack-boys exchanged fire. Both Don and his mans took it in slugs. Each of them lay twisted on the pavement, riddled with bullets. TJ and Bone hurried to collect both the bloodstained totes while Rob stripped Don of his Rolex. They noticed a female behind the tinted windows of the Range who'd witnessed the murderous robbery. It was Shanta. She let out a bloodcurdling scream.

Bone took aim at Shanta, but then TJ shoved him towards the SUV, and they turned for it. However, Rob took aim at the bitch and didn't hesitate to squeeze the trigger.

Boc!

After Rob's FN cracked once then Shanta's screams were silenced when the bullet shattered the window and then struck her. Rob then turned and hopped into the passenger seat of the SUV. The gang then skirted off, fishtailing out the parking lot, leaving Don and the others bleeding to death.

To Be Continued...
MONEY IN THE GRAVE 2
Coming Soon

Submission Guideline

Submit the first three chapters of your completed manuscript to ldpsubmissions@gmail.com, subject line: Your book's title. The manuscript must be in a .doc file and sent as an attachment. Document should be in Times New Roman, double spaced and in size 12 font. Also, provide your synopsis and full contact information. If sending multiple submissions, they must each be in a separate email.

Have a story but no way to send it electronically? You can still submit to LDP/Ca$h Presents. Send in the first three chapters, written or typed, of your completed manuscript to:

LDP: Submissions Dept
Po Box 944
Stockbridge, Ga 30281

DO NOT send original manuscript. Must be a duplicate.

Provide your synopsis and a cover letter containing your full contact information.

Thanks for considering LDP and Ca$h Presents.

Coming Soon from Lock Down Publications/Ca$h Presents

BOW DOWN TO MY GANGSTA

By **Ca$h**

TORN BETWEEN TWO

By **Coffee**

BLOOD OF A BOSS **VI**

SHADOWS OF THE GAME II

TRAP BASTARD II

By **Askari**

LOYAL TO THE GAME **IV**

By **T.J. & Jelissa**

IF LOVING YOU IS WRONG... **III**

By **Jelissa**

TRUE SAVAGE **VIII**

MIDNIGHT CARTEL IV

DOPE BOY MAGIC IV

CITY OF KINGZ III

By **Chris Green**

BLAST FOR ME **III**

A SAVAGE DOPEBOY III

CUTTHROAT MAFIA III

DUFFLE BAG CARTEL VII

HEARTLESS GOON VI

By **Ghost**

A HUSTLER'S DECEIT III

KILL ZONE **II**

Money in the Grave

BAE BELONGS TO ME III

A DOPE BOY'S QUEEN III

By **Aryanna**

COKE KINGS V

KING OF THE TRAP III

By **T.J. Edwards**

GORILLAZ IN THE BAY V

3X KRAZY III

De'Kari

THE STREETS ARE CALLING II

Duquie Wilson

KINGPIN KILLAZ IV

STREET KINGS III

PAID IN BLOOD III

CARTEL KILLAZ IV

DOPE GODS III

Hood Rich

SINS OF A HUSTLA II

ASAD

KINGZ OF THE GAME VI

Playa Ray

SLAUGHTER GANG IV

RUTHLESS HEART IV

By Willie Slaughter

FUK SHYT II

By Blakk Diamond

TRAP QUEEN

RICH $AVAGE II

MONEY IN THE GRAVE II

By Troublesome

YAYO V

GHOST MOB II

Stilloan Robinson

CREAM III

By Yolanda Moore

SON OF A DOPE FIEND III

HEAVEN GOT A GHETTO II

By Renta

FOREVER GANGSTA II

GLOCKS ON SATIN SHEETS III

By Adrian Dulan

LOYALTY AIN'T PROMISED III

By Keith Williams

THE PRICE YOU PAY FOR LOVE III

By Destiny Skai

I'M NOTHING WITHOUT HIS LOVE II

SINS OF A THUG II

TO THE THUG I LOVED BEFORE II

By Monet Dragun

LIFE OF A SAVAGE IV

MURDA SEASON IV

GANGLAND CARTEL IV

CHI'RAQ GANGSTAS IV

KILLERS ON ELM STREET IV

JACK BOYZ N DA BRONX III

A DOPEBOY'S DREAM II

By **Romell Tukes**

QUIET MONEY IV

EXTENDED CLIP III

THUG LIFE IV

By **Trai'Quan**

THE STREETS MADE ME III

By **Larry D. Wright**

IF YOU CROSS ME ONCE II

ANGEL III

By **Anthony Fields**

FRIEND OR FOE III

By **Mimi**

SAVAGE STORMS III

By **Meesha**

THE STREETS WILL NEVER CLOSE II

By **K'ajji**

IN THE ARM OF HIS BOSS

By **Jamila**

HARD AND RUTHLESS III

MOB TOWN 251 II

By Von Diesel

LEVELS TO THIS SHYT II

By Ah'Million

MOB TIES III

By SayNoMore

THE LAST OF THE OGS III
Tranay Adams
FOR THE LOVE OF A BOSS III
By C. D. Blue
MOBBED UP II
By King Rio
BRED IN THE GAME II
By S. Allen
KILLA KOUNTY II
By Khufu

Available Now

RESTRAINING ORDER **I & II**
By **CA$H & Coffee**
LOVE KNOWS NO BOUNDARIES **I II & III**
By **Coffee**
RAISED AS A GOON I, II, III & IV
BRED BY THE SLUMS I, II, III
BLAST FOR ME I & II
ROTTEN TO THE CORE I II III
A BRONX TALE I, II, III
DUFFLE BAG CARTEL I II III IV V VI
HEARTLESS GOON I II III IV V

Money in the Grave

A SAVAGE DOPEBOY I II

DRUG LORDS I II III

CUTTHROAT MAFIA I II

By **Ghost**

LAY IT DOWN **I & II**

LAST OF A DYING BREED I II

BLOOD STAINS OF A SHOTTA I & II III

By **Jamaica**

LOYAL TO THE GAME I II III

LIFE OF SIN I, II III

By **TJ & Jelissa**

BLOODY COMMAS I & II

SKI MASK CARTEL I II & III

KING OF NEW YORK I II,III IV V

RISE TO POWER I II III

COKE KINGS I II III IV

BORN HEARTLESS I II III IV

KING OF THE TRAP I II

By **T.J. Edwards**

IF LOVING HIM IS WRONG…I & II

LOVE ME EVEN WHEN IT HURTS I II III

By **Jelissa**

WHEN THE STREETS CLAP BACK I & II III

THE HEART OF A SAVAGE I II III

By **Jibril Williams**

A DISTINGUISHED THUG STOLE MY HEART I II & III

LOVE SHOULDN'T HURT I II III IV

Martell "Troublesome" Bolden

RENEGADE BOYS I II III IV
PAID IN KARMA I II III
SAVAGE STORMS I II
AN UNFORESEEN LOVE
By **Meesha**
A GANGSTER'S CODE I &, II III
A GANGSTER'S SYN I II III
THE SAVAGE LIFE I II III
CHAINED TO THE STREETS I II III
BLOOD ON THE MONEY I II III
By J-Blunt
PUSH IT TO THE LIMIT
By **Bre' Hayes**
BLOOD OF A BOSS **I, II, III, IV, V**
SHADOWS OF THE GAME
TRAP BASTARD
By **Askari**
THE STREETS BLEED MURDER **I, II & III**
THE HEART OF A GANGSTA I II& III
By **Jerry Jackson**
CUM FOR ME I II III IV V VI VII
An **LDP Erotica Collaboration**
BRIDE OF A HUSTLA **I II & II**
THE FETTI GIRLS **I, II& III**
CORRUPTED BY A GANGSTA I, II III, IV
BLINDED BY HIS LOVE
THE PRICE YOU PAY FOR LOVE I II

172

Money in the Grave

DOPE GIRL MAGIC I II III

By **Destiny Skai**

WHEN A GOOD GIRL GOES BAD

By **Adrienne**

THE COST OF LOYALTY I II III

By Kweli

A GANGSTER'S REVENGE **I II III & IV**

THE BOSS MAN'S DAUGHTERS I II III IV V

A SAVAGE LOVE **I & II**

BAE BELONGS TO ME I II

A HUSTLER'S DECEIT I, II, III

WHAT BAD BITCHES DO I, II, III

SOUL OF A MONSTER I II III

KILL ZONE

A DOPE BOY'S QUEEN I II

By **Aryanna**

A KINGPIN'S AMBITON

A KINGPIN'S AMBITION **II**

I MURDER FOR THE DOUGH

By **Ambitious**

TRUE SAVAGE I II III IV V VI VII

DOPE BOY MAGIC I, II, III

MIDNIGHT CARTEL I II III

CITY OF KINGZ I II

By **Chris Green**

A DOPEBOY'S PRAYER

By **Eddie "Wolf" Lee**

Martell "Troublesome" Bolden

THE KING CARTEL **I, II & III**
By **Frank Gresham**
THESE NIGGAS AIN'T LOYAL **I, II & III**
By **Nikki Tee**
GANGSTA SHYT **I II &III**
By **CATO**
THE ULTIMATE BETRAYAL
By **Phoenix**
BOSS'N UP **I , II & III**
By **Royal Nicole**
I LOVE YOU TO DEATH
By Destiny J
I RIDE FOR MY HITTA
I STILL RIDE FOR MY HITTA
By **Misty Holt**
LOVE & CHASIN' PAPER
By **Qay Crockett**
TO DIE IN VAIN
SINS OF A HUSTLA
By **ASAD**
BROOKLYN HUSTLAZ
By **Boogsy Morina**
BROOKLYN ON LOCK I & II
By **Sonovia**
GANGSTA CITY
By **Teddy Duke**
A DRUG KING AND HIS DIAMOND I & II III

Money in the Grave

A DOPEMAN'S RICHES

HER MAN, MINE'S TOO I, II

CASH MONEY HO'S

THE WIFEY I USED TO BE I II

By Nicole Goosby

TRAPHOUSE KING **I II & III**

KINGPIN KILLAZ I II III

STREET KINGS I II

PAID IN BLOOD **I II**

CARTEL KILLAZ I II III

DOPE GODS I II

By **Hood Rich**

LIPSTICK KILLAH **I, II, III**

CRIME OF PASSION I II & III

FRIEND OR FOE I II

By **Mimi**

STEADY MOBBN' **I, II, III**

THE STREETS STAINED MY SOUL I II

By **Marcellus Allen**

WHO SHOT YA **I, II, III**

SON OF A DOPE FIEND I II

HEAVEN GOT A GHETTO

Renta

GORILLAZ IN THE BAY **I II III IV**

TEARS OF A GANGSTA I II

3X KRAZY I II

DE'KARI

Martell "Troublesome" Bolden

TRIGGADALE I II III
Elijah R. Freeman
GOD BLESS THE TRAPPERS I, II, III
THESE SCANDALOUS STREETS I, II, III
FEAR MY GANGSTA I, II, III IV, V
THESE STREETS DON'T LOVE NOBODY I, II
BURY ME A G I, II, III, IV, V
A GANGSTA'S EMPIRE I, II, III, IV
THE DOPEMAN'S BODYGAURD I II
THE REALEST KILLAZ I II III
THE LAST OF THE OGS I II
Tranay Adams
THE STREETS ARE CALLING
Duquie Wilson
MARRIED TO A BOSS... I II III
By Destiny Skai & Chris Green
KINGZ OF THE GAME I II III IV V
Playa Ray
SLAUGHTER GANG I II III
RUTHLESS HEART I II III
By Willie Slaughter
FUK SHYT
By Blakk Diamond
DON'T F#CK WITH MY HEART I II
By Linnea
ADDICTED TO THE DRAMA I II III
IN THE ARM OF HIS BOSS II

Money in the Grave

By Jamila

YAYO I II III IV

A SHOOTER'S AMBITION I II

BRED IN THE GAME

By S. Allen

TRAP GOD I II III

RICH $AVAGE

MONEY IN THE GRAVE

By Troublesome

FOREVER GANGSTA

GLOCKS ON SATIN SHEETS I II

By Adrian Dulan

TOE TAGZ I II III

LEVELS TO THIS SHYT

By Ah'Million

KINGPIN DREAMS I II III

By Paper Boi Rari

CONFESSIONS OF A GANGSTA I II III

By Nicholas Lock

I'M NOTHING WITHOUT HIS LOVE

SINS OF A THUG

TO THE THUG I LOVED BEFORE

By Monet Dragun

CAUGHT UP IN THE LIFE I II III

By Robert Baptiste

NEW TO THE GAME I II III

MONEY, MURDER & MEMORIES I II III

By **Malik D. Rice**

LIFE OF A SAVAGE I II III

A GANGSTA'S QUR'AN I II III

MURDA SEASON I II III

GANGLAND CARTEL I II III

CHI'RAQ GANGSTAS I II III

KILLERS ON ELM STREET I II III

JACK BOYZ N DA BRONX I II

A DOPEBOY'S DREAM

By **Romell Tukes**

LOYALTY AIN'T PROMISED I II

By Keith Williams

QUIET MONEY I II III

THUG LIFE I II III

EXTENDED CLIP I II

By **Trai'Quan**

THE STREETS MADE ME I II

By **Larry D. Wright**

THE ULTIMATE SACRIFICE I, II, III, IV, V, VI

KHADIFI

IF YOU CROSS ME ONCE

ANGEL I II

IN THE BLINK OF AN EYE

By **Anthony Fields**

THE LIFE OF A HOOD STAR

By Ca$h & Rashia Wilson

Money in the Grave

THE STREETS WILL NEVER CLOSE

By K'ajji

CREAM I II

By Yolanda Moore

NIGHTMARES OF A HUSTLA I II III

By King Dream

CONCRETE KILLA I II

By Kingpen

HARD AND RUTHLESS I II

MOB TOWN 251

By Von Diesel

GHOST MOB II

Stilloan Robinson

MOB TIES I II

By SayNoMore

BODYMORE MURDERLAND I II III

By Delmont Player

FOR THE LOVE OF A BOSS I II

By C. D. Blue

MOBBED UP

By King Rio

KILLA KOUNTY

By Khufu

BOOKS BY LDP'S CEO, CA$H

TRUST IN NO MAN

TRUST IN NO MAN 2

TRUST IN NO MAN 3

BONDED BY BLOOD

SHORTY GOT A THUG

THUGS CRY

THUGS CRY 2

THUGS CRY 3

TRUST NO BITCH

TRUST NO BITCH 2

TRUST NO BITCH 3

TIL MY CASKET DROPS

RESTRAINING ORDER

RESTRAINING ORDER 2

IN LOVE WITH A CONVICT

LIFE OF A HOOD STAR

Money in the Grave

9 781955 270373